Shit Happens in Ivydell

Indie Sparks

Twice Shy Publishing

PLEASE READ BEFORE PROCEEDING

Welcome back to Ivydell. Though this story takes place in a fictional desert community and no scorpion will spring from the pages to sting you, there are some things here that could cause harm, and I want you to be aware of them before you proceed.

In book 1, Where the Hell is Ivy Dell?, grief touches the characters. During this leg of the journey, it sucker punches a character. If you've ever battled grief, you know it doesn't fight fair. It's unpredictable. The grief in these pages is no kinder.

If you are currently struggling with grief, remember, there is a way forward. Please know that if you choose to read this book, there is always going to be a way forward for these characters as well. But that may not be enough to shield you from harm at this time. Take care of yourself. The book will be here if you're ready for it later. Your own story matters more than any book.

This book also features a frank conversation about a past car accident that left no survivors. There is a way forward, even from a seemingly insurmountable loss as this. Even when you can't find it with your high beams, it's there. There is a way forward for the fictional character who lost so much as well. Revealing this detail about the accident is not really a spoiler. In fact, you may have figured it out while reading book 1. If not, learning it here will not ruin the experience of reading this book.

There is so much more to the story.

Presumably, you've read book 1, Where the Hell is Ivy Dell?, but if you haven't, close this book right now, and go read that one. You are in the wrong place, but you can come back.

~

With that out of the way, this book is for everyone who read book 1 and is ready for more. Welcome back to Ivydell! Your casita awaits.

~

Ready your snacks. Remember to hydrate. Recharge anything that needs recharging during the angsty scenes because there might be more spice ahead. I could give you the exact page number where Jensen's dick makes its final appearance. But we both know I'm not going to.

~

And, full disclosure (this means you can't yell at me later and say I misled you): No, all your questions will not be answered in this book either. Calm your tits, gorgeous! There are two more books to come after this one. We'll get there together.

~

Turn the page. It's go time!

Ivy

The Preparation Begins

CUJO WAS THE FIRST resident to come back to Ivydell after Jensen and I had the whole compound to ourselves for a few days. We expected to be alone at least another day before anyone returned, and Cujo was supposed to be gone for a few weeks. But he rode right past Jensen's casita—newly named *Vintage Vibes*, courtesy of me—and gave us the rest of our expected alone time.

Somehow, I'm not convinced Cujo is really the loner outlaw people think he is. I think there might be a big teddy bear under that long beard and leather vest. But I recognize the name of the motorcycle club on his patches, and they're not known for being teddy bears.

Jensen says Cujo is more of an auxiliary member, though he admits he doesn't know exactly what that means and doesn't want to.

Ivydell's unspoken policy of not questioning your neighbors has its merits. There are some things you're better off not knowing. Live and let live.

Petra and the Spirit Sisters, more officially known as Alma and Elma, along with Myrna, Ivydell's resident purveyor of shiny obscenities, all came back this morning.

I got a text from Petra shortly after their arrival. It was an invitation to help with some prep for the annual arts festival that Ivydell will host next month. I'm only a temporary resident, so I'm not expected to contribute at the same level as everyone else, but it feels nice to be included. I came here to find out more about this place, and as the seasonal residents come back, I know more questions will be answered.

The more I interact, the more I'll learn.

Jensen honks the horn of his truck as he drives by my place on his way to Cujo's casita. I smile at the sound as I fill my tumbler with coffee.

Cool, crisp air greets me when I step outside. The wind is calm right now, so there's no blowing dirt to assault my clean hair. I've twisted it up into a clip because it will be coated with desert dust soon enough, regardless.

My next-door neighbor, Josephine, is still gone. It's weird to miss someone you hardly know, but aside from Jensen, she's the only other resident close to my age.

I wonder if she knows Cujo is back already. She's more than neighborly with him.

Myrna waves from across the dirt road that separates our casitas. She's wearing rubber boots and has a pair of gardening gloves in her hand. The sneakers I'm wearing are the most casual shoes I brought with me, and I definitely didn't bring any type of work gloves. Hopefully, whatever we're doing today won't involve getting too intimate with cactus thorns.

Jensen probably has some gloves I can borrow. But then again, Petra probably does, too. I can't expect to rely on him for every little thing I need, even if he has been exceedingly good at meeting all my needs so far . . .

Lost in my thoughts of our past few days together, I don't realize Myrna has crossed the road until she's right in front of me. She's short and thin, but she has a big energy about her; not to mention her big silver jewelry that catches the mid-morning sun and causes me to squint.

Squinting is always the safer way to view her pieces because you never know what you might find depicted in her curlicues. She's a master silversmith and jewelry maker. Her work is detailed. Complex. And sometimes, a little disturbing for me. But she's fun.

"Are we gardening today? I don't have any tools. Or gloves."

"Don't worry, doll. Petra will have what you need."

Of course. Petra, the fairy godmother of Ivydell, love of Gran's life, and the reason I'm here. She's the only one who can fill in the blanks for me about why Gran loved this remote and rustic place so much. And why she wouldn't come back.

As expected, Petra greets us when we round the curve to her place by waving gloves in the air. "Hope you gals are ready to work!"

I look down at my nails. My last trip to the nail salon was over three weeks ago and it shows. There are so many little things I didn't think about before I gassed up my car and hit the road. But I'm not sorry to be here. How could I be when Jensen kisses the way he does? Not to mention the other skilled acts his mouth performs. And the rest of his skills.

Okay, time to shake off all thoughts of Jensen. Or this is going to be a long day in the sun.

"What are we planting?"

Petra and Myrna laugh. That happens a lot around here—I say something that makes someone laugh, even though I don't know why it's funny.

"No planting. We're clearing and cleaning the pathways. The festival is in less than a month." Petra hands me a rake. "Now that I know you enjoy planting, I'll remember to let you help with that when the time comes."

I'm not sure I'd say I enjoy it, but it sounds better than raking dirt.

Myrna snickers. "Your back is going to be sore tonight, girlie. Maybe Stinger will give you a massage."

Petra's glare could slice through steel. I'm still not sure which one of us she wants to protect more, me or Jensen. I'm even more confused by what she thought would happen when I met him. She's a lesbian, but she's not blind. That man is a sight to behold. And a joy to hold as well. My closed hand slides a few inches up and down on the rake handle before I can stop it.

I'm pretty sure I'm the only one who noticed my attempt to jack a rake. I smile, thinking about how Jensen actually is a rake, or he probably was in a past life. Maybe he still is, whether that's the current term for it or not. Maybe that's why Petra worries about me spending time with him.

She doesn't need to worry about me. I can handle whatever I'm getting myself into with him.

Jensen

A Shift in the Wind

I PULL UP TO Cujo's place and find him repacking a toolbox. "Anything I can help with?"

"Nah, all done. You've got good timing."

"For once. You didn't stay gone long."

He shakes his head. "Plans got canceled."

That's all he offers, so I let it go. Of all the people who live in Ivydell, I wonder about him the most. I used to tell myself when he took off for weeks at a time, it was probably to be with a woman. But now that he's seeing Josephine, I don't know.

It's none of my business, and technically, I'm not sure what his arrangement is with Josephine, but they seem like a good match. Some people just fit.

"Surprised Petra doesn't have you busy already," he says. "She's been back for hours, and you know how she gets this close to the festival."

"I might be avoiding her."

He throws his head back and laughs. "We both know that's not possible. If she wanted you, she'd have found you already."

"True. You want to go fishing?"

"I'm not doing anything else."

I help Cujo gather his fishing gear and load it into the bed of my truck. Taking the long way around was an attempt to avoid seeing Petra, but there she is, realigning stones along a walkway that cuts through the center of Ivydell and leads back to The Circle.

That rock border has to be cleaned up and reset every year because the wind blows leaves and debris in between them, and they get knocked around by animals. The path will have to be cleaned again right before the festival, but doing the worst of the work now makes it easier.

Ivy rakes the pathway clean, her leggings tight enough that I can make out the shape of the muscles in her legs . . . and the curve of her firm, round ass. No wonder Petra hasn't recruited me to help. She wants me and Ivy to stay as far away from each other as possible.

Plus, it's easier to get volunteers to help now. The closer the festival gets, the busier everybody gets with their own preparations. In another few weeks, there will be artists working everywhere you look.

Cujo's eyes follow the same outlines of Ivy's body as mine, and my fingers tighten around the steering wheel.

"Hope you didn't exhaust her too much over the past few days. Petra will keep her out here all day."

"Anything to keep her away from me."

"Why is that?"

"Pretty sure she doesn't think I'm good enough for her."

"You're not."

"Thanks."

"Hell, it's anybody's guess what Josephine sees in me. But I'm going to keep coming around until she tells me to stop."

"What if she never tells you to stop?"

It's rare to see a smile light up Cujo's face. He'll laugh now and then, but he's not a smiley guy.

"Who the fuck knows?" he says with a shrug.

Shadow's car pulls in the gate as I'm pulling up in front of the shops. He waves through the windshield, but doesn't slow down to chat.

"Looks like everybody's coming back sooner than they'd planned." Cujo rolls down his window and waves back.

"I don't understand why Shadow doesn't leave during the festival. He hates it, but he's always here for it."

Cujo gives me another nonchalant shrug. "Maybe there's someone who used to be a regular, and he's always hoping they'll show up again."

"Is that the deal? You know there's someone he's hoping will come back?"

"I don't know shit, man. I'm just talking."

"Right." I hop out and grab my fishing pole and tackle box from inside the shop. The wind changes direction. It's early March and there's another cool front headed our way. It's warm enough to fish in a t-shirt today, but we might all be wearing jackets again tomorrow. Maybe before the day's over. I grab one off a hook by the door, just in case.

The elderly twin mediums walk past as I climb back in my truck. Cujo waves to them, too. He's in a damn good mood today.

"You ever talk to the Spirit Sisters?" he asks. "They're a trip."

"Not if I can help it. I call them the spooky sisters because they creep me the fuck out."

"They know some crazy shit sometimes. I used to think psychics were all a scam, but they've told me some stuff . . ." He trails off, and frankly, I'm glad.

"You going to be weird all day?"

"I haven't decided yet."

He sits taller in the seat. The spread of his shoulders reminds me just how much bigger he is than me. I'm always aware when we lift weights together, but outside the building that says plumbing on the front, where we keep our equipment—and old bench and disc weights, some dumbbells, and a kettlebell that neither of us ever picks up—he seems less intimidating. Usually.

We drive past two more seasonal residents returning to Ivydell. More waves are exchanged through the windshield.

I better enjoy fishing today. By tomorrow, they'll all have punch lists of things for me to fix or replace. Staying busy is good. Keeps all the *what-ifs* at bay. Mostly.

Ivy

Judging a Bottle by Its Label

MY SHOWER MAY BE small, but the water is hot. And the heat feels incredible on my aching shoulders. When Petra says we're having a workday, I now know she means a *work* day. I'm happy to be here and happy to contribute where I can, but damn, when I let her put that rake in my hand, I didn't fully realize what I was getting into.

I got to watch prairie dogs play, and we didn't see any rattlesnakes or scorpions, so it definitely could've been worse. But the time didn't exactly fly by. Unfortunately, Petra is not a talk-while-she-works woman.

Myrna, on the other hand, had plenty to say. Petra watched her like a hawk, though. Every time Myrna brought up Jensen, whom she, like everybody else here, calls Stinger, Petra would cock her head like a warning.

What wasn't she supposed to say in front of me?

She said enough that I know he came here after a major heartbreak. I knew something traumatic had to have happened, but he told me he inherited his family's winery, so I assumed his parents died and that was the reason he ended up here.

Myrna definitely made it sound like his heart was devastated by more than the loss of his parents.

I've had my heart broken, too, and it's not like I thought I was the first woman he'd ever spent time with, but I'm feeling weirdly jealous of the unknown.

No, that's not it, not jealous. But I feel like I have a right to know what happened in his life, which I don't.

This unwarranted entitlement to his history keeps nagging at me, though. I can't help it; I want to know everything about him. He's more intriguing than anyone I've ever known, and I hardly know anything at all.

What if there's something terrible in his past? Something that would make me not want to be around him anymore. It would have to be something pretty bad to quell my infatuation with him.

Sweet goddess, I hate admitting that, even to myself.

I breathe in the lavender-scented steam of my shower and try to decide if there's anything in my history that I wouldn't want him to know. Every memory I call up feels like it would be safe with him. I can't imagine him judging me for any of my past fuck-ups or embarrassing moments.

Teasing me, sure. But despite his initial gruffness, he's one of the most easygoing people I've ever met. So accepting. Adaptable.

Damn, Gran would've loved him.

Tears slip from my eyes, taking me by surprise. It happens a lot in the shower, especially when I let myself think about hard stuff. The shower has always been where I process and work through things. The steam clears more than my sinuses sometimes.

Usually, crying in the shower feels cathartic; today, it feels pathetic. I turn off the water and grab a towel. It's early for pajamas, but I don't plan to go out again. My bed is already calling. I slip into a soft tank top and climb between the sheets.

It's a good time to check in with Mom. Still rush hour at home, so the emergency room might be too busy for her to reply. I don't want her to worry, but she didn't support my plan to spend a few months here, and her disapproval comes across loud and clear in her messages sometimes.

She hates Ivydell, and my not hating it is not what she'd hoped for.

> Hey, hope you're having a good day. Just wanted to say hi. Love you!

> Is the wind bad there today?

> No. It's been beautiful. I helped Petra and Myrna clean up the path to The Circle. My arms feel like I've been lifting weights all day. All I did was rake. Guess I need to do more arm days at the gym.

> No gym in Ivydell.

> No, but I'm getting exercise. My gym membership will still be there when I get back.

> You did pause it, right? You're not paying for the months you're not even here, are you?

> It's all good, Mom. Didn't you have a date this weekend? How'd it go?

> I'll tell you about it later. Ambulance en route. Love you.

She could at least tell me if her date went well or not. I'm guessing not.

I haven't told her everything lately either. Didn't mention the scorpion sting. Or the badger on my back patio. Or the mountain lion that visited.

Or Jensen.

I'm debating whether I want to text him and invite him over. I ate a peanut butter sandwich before I showered. He eats late sometimes, and I don't have anything decent here to offer him. I for sure don't want to go anywhere, not even for the fourth best barbecue in the state. But the memory brings a quick smile to my face.

There's a hard slap on my door that makes me jump. And then the knob jiggles and a familiar voice follows. "Open up! I know you're in there."

Josephine. She shouldn't be back yet. Why are everyone's plans changing?

I scramble out of bed and into a pair of shorts and open the door. Her dark curls are held behind her ears by the arms of her sunglasses, which are sitting on top of her head. The blue of her eyes is always arresting, but with her hair pulled back, I can't look away from them. Until she holds up a black nylon bag. "You gonna let me in or what?"

"Well, I was, but now, I'm not sure. What is that?"

"I had four clients cancel on me. Four! I've never had that many in a row. I need to put some ink in some skin. And I choose yours."

"That explains why you're back from Albuquerque early."

"Yep." She sets the bag on my bed. "What do you want? Flowers? Butterfly?"

"I never said I wanted a tattoo, but if I did, how do you know I wouldn't choose something edgier than flowers or butterflies?"

"I am not doing a chipmunk tattoo."

"Don't want that either."

"How about a scorpion?" She waggles her eyebrows at me.

"Oh, sure. It wouldn't be weird at all to get the same tattoo as Jensen."

"You could get yours somewhere more interesting than your neck."

"No scorpion."

"Come on, Ivy! You're too old not to have any tattoos. How'd you grow up at the beach and remain ink-free? Didn't all your friends have tats?"

"No, not all of them. I almost got one once, but I chickened out. My mom's a nurse. She fed me horror stories about them my whole life. Allergic reactions. Infections." I shrug. "I got over it."

"What were you going to get?"

"A strand of ivy that wrapped around my ankle and extended onto the top of my foot."

She flinches. "Thank God you didn't go through with that."

"What's wrong with it?"

"It's not very interesting. Basic. Boring."

"If I said yes to you, which I'm not, what would you suggest?"

"What about a tribute to your Gran? Something from her art-work?"

"Huh. I never thought about that. It could be a tribute to her and my time in Ivydell."

"See? I knew we'd come up with something."

"No."

"What do you mean, no?"

"I don't want a tattoo. I was just saying if I did, that would be a good idea."

A resounding knock interrupts before she can respond. I know who is on the other side of the door before I open it this time, too.

He's also freshly showered, even wearing a shirt. But his scorpion tail is visible above his collar. It still draws my eyes every time I see it.

"Am I interrupting girls' night?"

"Yes!" Josephine shouts, simultaneously to me saying no.

Jensen laughs until he spots the black bag on the bed. "You setting up shop?"

Josephine's head bobs excitedly. "Yes. Want some new ink?"

"Maybe."

How is this happening? I didn't say my casita could be turned into a tattoo shop. That's a terrible idea, anyway. I'm well acquainted with my housekeeping habits. There's no way it's sanitary enough in here. I haven't dusted once since I arrived over two weeks ago.

"No way. I'm not going to be responsible for him getting an infection and having to have a limb amputated."

"Excuse me!" Josephine pulls her head back dramatically. "Nobody has ever had to have anything amputated because of one of my tattoos."

"This isn't a sterile environment."

She looks around like she sees nothing wrong with the space. "His skin will be sterile, and so will my gun. The needles are pre-sterilized and disposable. There's not debris flying around, so trust me, it'll be fine."

"I trust you," Jensen says, pulling his shirt off as if it's been decided.

Clearly, they've both lost their minds. "But there probably is stuff flying around. Just because you can't see contaminates doesn't mean they're not here. There are germs everywhere!"

Josephine unzips her bag and splays it open, revealing her tattoo machine, little containers of ink, paper, pencils, and other things I can't make out before she leans over it and blocks my line of sight. She pulls out a small bottle and heads for my kitchen sink, where she washes her hands with her own cleanser.

If she doesn't even trust my soap . . .

"Listen," she says, drying her hands with her own cloth, too. "When I go to conferences in convention halls, do you think those places are sterile? I don't need an operating room. This is fine."

"Do you want me to lean on the counter or lie on the bed?"

They're just going to proceed like my opinion doesn't matter? I live here!

"Maybe I don't want his blood all over my bed. Did anybody think about that?"

Jensen smiles. "How much blood do you think is spilled when someone gets a tattoo?"

"For real," Josephine says. "He won't bleed onto any surface. I'll be wiping the blood as I go. You never even went with a friend when they got a tattoo?"

"No. I was always afraid if I went, they'd pressure me into getting one."

"You don't strike me as an easy target for peer pressure." She stretches gloves onto her hands. "I mean, if I can't convince you to get one, I don't see anybody else getting through to you."

"Not now. But fitting in was really important to me at one

point." I bite my lip, wishing I hadn't just revealed that. Jensen and Josephine probably never cared about being part of a crowd. They both have that lone wolf thing going on—not like creepy loners, more like people who are confident enough not to give a damn what anyone else thinks about their choices. I envy it.

I'm more that way now than I've ever been, but I still didn't tell anybody other than Mom that I was coming here. It wasn't because I didn't care what they'd think; it was because I was afraid that they'd talk me out of it, or at least make me question it until I talked myself out of it.

Some of my friends are probably in a group chat right now because they've seen my pics on social media. I can just hear them talking shit about how I've gone off the deep end and run away to the desert. For all I know, they're planning an intervention. A rescue mission.

But I've never been happier to have made a rash decision in my life. Aside from the impending tattoo session I'm about to witness, I've felt completely at home here.

"What do you want, and where do you want it?"

"I don't know." Jensen cocks his head. "Probably my shoulder. Something related to Ivydell. We don't have a sign, but Bear Rock, maybe?"

"Love the rock. Don't want to tattoo it on you. Let's do something more vibrant."

"What about something to do with wine?" I say, impaling the cork in an unopened bottle with my corkscrew.

"No." His response is quick. And harsh.

"Sit in this chair." Josephine pulls out one of my bistro chairs and turns it around so the back is braced against the edge of the small table.

He settles his bare chest into the back of my chair, wrapping his forearms around it and letting them rest on the tabletop, while Josephine wipes his shoulder clean and stares at his skin, tilting her head from side to side like she's envisioning what she should immortalize there.

What I wouldn't give to be that chair right now, wrapped in his strong arms with his chest pressed against me. I fumble a wine glass as I take it out of the cabinet, but I manage to steady it on the counter without breaking it.

Jensen sees my struggle and smiles. Adorable klutz isn't really the way I want him to see me right now, but his smile makes it clear that's exactly what he's thinking. Josephine can't see anything but his tight, tanned skin she's about to adorn with fresh ink.

"I wish Ivydell did have a sign. I could work with that, add some cactus and maybe a rattlesnake . . ."

"Vintage Vibes needs a sign." I pour myself some wine, and don't offer them any since they obviously can't drink it right now. More for me.

"That's true." Jensen nods, his voice softer at this suggestion.

Josephine crinkles her nose and knits her brows into a confused expression as she lays things out on a metal tray she's sterilized and covered with a disposable pad. She doesn't know what we're talking about. Until this moment, that was an inside thing between Jensen and me.

"She named my place Vintage Vibes."

"His was the only one without a name." I take a sip of my wine. "It bugged me."

"So, it's actually the perfect image," Jensen says. "You create the sign for the tattoo, and then someone can make it in real life to go in front of my casita. Then they'll all officially have names, and Ivy can sleep at night."

He smiles at me again, adds a wink to be sure I know he's not being an asshole. There's no doubt the man can be grumpy, and sometimes he comes across hard, but I'm learning to read him. I already knew he was teasing, but that wink reassures me of other things—most prominent among them is my desire to climb him like a tree right now.

"No pressure. Thanks." Josephine releases a resigned, heavy breath. "I was going to do this freehand, but not now."

She pulls her gloves off and throws them away. Then she takes a piece of paper and pencil from her bag and sits in the other chair at my table.

"Want a glass of wine while she sketches?"

"What are you drinking?"

I hesitantly turn the label toward him. It's not from Hilltop, the fancy little market with the great wine selection where he buys his. I'd feel weird going there without him. If the owner, Shane, recognized me, I'm afraid he'd assume I know about wine like Jensen does, and he'd start speaking in that foreign wine-guy talk to me.

Sometimes, I read the little tag on the shelf beneath a bottle with ratings or notes, but not all bottles have that. Mostly, my buying choices are driven by the label and the price tag.

Tonight's selection is called Savage Daughter, and it has a witchy looking woman with flowers in her hair, rising from a swamp on the label. It's a cabernet sauvignon. Pretty bottle, and the price was closer to fifteen than twenty. Instabuy.

"Is it any good?" he asks.

"I like it."

"Then it's good, Ivy. If you like it, it's good."

"Yeah, but you're probably going to tell me what's bad about it as soon as you taste it."

He looks at his empty hand, curved as if it's holding an invisible wine glass. "So far, it doesn't seem like I'm going to get the opportunity."

"Fine." I pour him a glass and take it to the table.

Of course, he swirls it a few times and watches the crimson liquid rise and fall, and then he brings the glass to his nose and inhales. He's a wine guy, but I think there's a fair chance he's doing this to fuck with me.

Finally, he takes a sip, lets it linger on his tongue before he swallows. "Not bad for a wine you bought just because you liked the label."

"That's not true. I also considered the price."

His smile widens. "You did all right."

"But you'd have done better."

"Maybe, maybe not. Trying a new wine with no recommendation is a gamble."

"How do you choose in that situation? When there's no little notecard on the shelf and you've never heard of it, how do you decide?"

"Sometimes I'm forced to judge a bottle by its label."

"Liar."

"Not entirely. But I meant I *read* the label, not buy it based on the artwork."

"Guess it's a good thing I got lucky."

"Guess that makes me lucky by association."

"Can I claim to be a sommelier by association?"

His smile fades a little. "I'm not a sommelier."

Whatever I just triggered, I wish I could undo it. His deep, flirty voice rarely goes flat like that. Toneless. Emotionless. I like it better when he's agitated. At least there's some passion in that. Right now, he sounds . . . lifeless.

"You could be one, though."

"Yeah. If I wanted to pursue that, I could." His smile brightens, but there's a veil of sadness in his eyes. He'll blink it away soon. He always does. But I see it there. And I wish I could ask about it without feeling like I'm intruding where I don't belong.

Josephine slides the drawing she's been working on over a few inches for his opinion.

"Come look," he says.

"It's not going on my body. My opinion isn't the one that matters."

"It matters to me."

Josephines eyes widen, and she bites back a smile. She shrugs at me. "Sounds like you better weigh in on this."

I step close enough to see what she's drawn. The sign is a board nailed to two posts, the same style as all the existing signs. There is a pair of burrowing owls at the base of one post, and a cluster of prickly pear cactus surrounding the other.

Those little owls remind me of the hissing sound that interrupted us in The Circle when everyone was away and we were the only two people left in Ivydell. The way he'd stared at me, admired my nakedness under a starry sky. What was it he said? Something about wanting to be able to recall every inch of me after I'd left this place. And then he bent me over and gave me the opportunity to memorize every inch of his dick, stretching me as he thrust deeper into my pussy in the cool, dark desert night. That scene plays out in my head like something from a movie. Like a dream.

Shit. I'm supposed to be giving feedback on Josephine's drawing, not reliving Jensen railing me in The Circle like we were performing some sacred ceremony. I force my eyes to focus on the sketch.

"Why'd you put that little bird sitting on it instead of a hawk?"

"It's a sparrow." She says it like she can't believe I didn't get that.

"Is that ivy?" I lean in. "It doesn't grow wild here."

She and Jensen exchange a look. And then a smile.

"I like it." He sets his wineglass on the table and pushes it toward me to be sure it's out of the way before he resumes his earlier position. "Let's do it."

Jensen

The Bristles Mean Nothing

WHY IS MY PHONE buzzing like a bug zapper? It's too early for this many people to be trying to reach me. The room is still mostly dark. Dim, anyway.

I roll over to check the notifications—right onto my right shoulder. The one with the new tattoo. That's annoying as fuck. Pushing up onto my right forearm, I extend my left hand and grab my damn phone. This requires entirely too much thought.

My vision is blurry because my eyes know we should still be asleep. Ivy stirs next to me, but her eyes remain closed. I swear she could sleep through a tornado.

She sleeps soundly, but not motionless. After a night of squirming and flip-flopping from her stomach to her back, her hair is a mess. An extremely cute mess. Her mouth is slightly open and her little kitten snores make me want to ignore my phone and pull her warm body next to mine.

Another notification lights up my screen. Fine, goddammit.

Oh. The coffee shop is reopening today. I forgot about seeing Tawny and Leo drive in right after Shadow. But, of course, they're up early and ready to greet everyone with a hot cup of strong coffee from who knows where. They pick up new varieties everywhere they go, mostly from independent roasters and shops.

You never know if you're going to taste pecan or chicory or chocolate.

"Wake up, sleepyhead." I trail my fingertip down the slope of Ivy's nose and over her cheekbone.

She wiggles, swats at my hand, and slurs unintelligibly.

"Come on. We're going to get coffee."

"There's coffee in my kitchen."

"I know, but the coffee shop is open."

"I don't want to drive half an hour for coffee. I want to sleep."

"We're not driving. We're walking."

That wakes her up. She sits with her head lolled to the side and rubs her eyes. "What the hell did you just say?"

Her raspy morning voice reawakens my morning wood. The way her nipples strain against the thin fabric of her tank top makes me want to occupy my mouth with those instead of coffee. But if we don't get down there soon, someone will come pounding on the door.

"Let's go before they come get us."

"Are you okay?" She rubs sleep from her eyes, looking at me like she thinks she might be dreaming this entire conversation.

I realize how crazy this sounds to her. What coffee shop? Where? She doesn't understand how it works.

"Tawny and Leo are married. Both artists. They travel all over, supporting small businesses as they go by buying coffee. They bring it back here and set up a café in the community center. Today is the grand reopening. We have to go. It's tradition."

"Oh, yeah. Petra said the community center is also a coffee shop. I forgot about that."

Fortunately, she's intrigued. She's not a morning person, so the appeal of regional coffees must be strong. But just to be sure she stays interested, I add, "Also, Tawny bakes."

"There's a bakery onsite now?" Her legs fly over the edge of the bed, and she practically sprints to the bathroom. "Yes!"

She's ready to go in five minutes. I splash water on my face and wish I had a toothbrush here. "Any chance you have an extra toothbrush?"

"Yeah. There's a pack of them in the drawer."

I slide the drawer open and see the opened package with three new toothbrushes left. They're all black, including the bristles.

"Did you buy these at Halloween?"

"They have charcoal built into the bristles. It helps to whiten your teeth."

Bullshit. "Did you pay extra for that feature? Because I'm pretty sure that's just a marketing ploy."

She appears in the doorway, moving her index finger up and down rapidly in front of her mouth. "Brush more, talk less. I need coffee."

I don't want to dampen her cheery mood, so I keep my thoughts to myself and use her bullshit charcoal toothbrush. She walks away with a smile on her face. I'd brush my teeth with an actual chunk of charcoal to see that.

She comes back into the bathroom as I'm rinsing and spitting. She's holding a knife.

"I promise not to disrespect your toothbrushes again. Don't stab."

With a halfhearted laugh, she notches a sliver of plastic from the handle of the one I just used. "There. Now we'll know which one is yours."

Okay. So, I have a toothbrush at her place now. That's . . . more impactful than it should be. Why does that feel like a momentous change?

I stare at the two toothbrushes in the holder.

His and hers.

Side by side.

Yeah, I need coffee.

Ivy is talkative the whole walk. She is so excited about the chipmunks emerging from hibernation. She's anti-love, but pro-rodent. I'm almost looking forward to the little bastards running amok again just to see her reaction to them.

"Did you put that ointment on your tattoo this morning like Josephine told you to?"

"Yes." It's been a long time since anyone has cared about something like that where I'm concerned. A long time since I've wanted anyone to.

"You're lying."

"Why do think I'm lying?"

"You have a tell. Everyone does. Mine is a lip twitch."

"Good to know. But I don't have one."

"Yes, you do. Your eyes get big like a cartoon character for just a split second."

She opens her eyes as wide as they'll go for the alleged split second to demonstrate.

"My eyes have never done that."

"You also didn't use that ointment this morning."

"I'll do it later. It's fine." I take her hand and squeeze. "How'd you know?"

"I'm not sure. I just knew."

She swings our hands, causing my shirt to rub against the fresh ink on my shoulder that I didn't moisturize this morning. It's agitating, but it makes me smile. She just knew.

Looks like we're the last arrivals at the coffee shop. All eyes are on us when we walk in together. A few people lift their mugs to say hello.

Petra's mouth becomes a hard line.

A hard no.

Not that she can stop us, but she would if she could. I don't understand her concern. Ivy's grieving, but she's not fragile. I've been single and never apologized for acting it, but I'm not an uncaring asshole. I keep telling myself it's not about me, but damn. It sure feels personal when she looks at me that way.

She doesn't know all there is to know about me. And I understand her less every time she expresses her disapproval of me spending time with Ivy.

Sometimes, the way we don't ask questions around here just creates more.

Ivy

Caffeine, Sugar & Hope

OKAY, I DIDN'T THINK I missed anything about my life back home, but being in the community center this morning reminds me how much I thrive on being around people. I've always enjoyed working remote, but I see people socially.

In Ivydell, I've spent a little time with Petra and Josephine, a little more with Jensen. I've even had coffee with Myrna, but aside from Jensen, it's all been brief, and not everyone is around all the time here.

This is nice. Community, like the sign says.

Some days back at home, I take my computer to a local coffee shop for a few hours so I can be around people while I work. It's not like being in the office. The people working at the other tables aren't my coworkers. No one is going to come over to vent about the company, or ask me to help them with anything. We're just busy people, sharing our energy and the occasional casual conversation.

I might be a little conversation deprived at this point because I've asked Tawny a hundred questions about the places they've been since they were last in Ivydell. She's eager to share stories, so I think maybe she's missed this, too.

Leo requests everyone's attention so he can explain the blend we're all currently drinking. He tells us about the young couple who own the farm in California where the beans were grown and how they roast them.

Tomorrow, he's going to wow us all with roasted cacao, but he promises there will be regular coffee available, too. He says he has a lot of new things to introduce, and we can check our skepticism at the door. The mild laughter in the room is accompanied by a few groans, Myrna's being the loudest.

She says she likes her coffee plain and simple.

Unlike her jewelry.

I can't wait to try the brewed cacao. Iffy on Leo's enthusiasm for mushroom coffee, though. I've tried it once, and it was so bitter it brought tears to my eyes. Leo assures me I'll be impressed. Tawny makes a yuck face behind his back.

They're probably in their early sixties, two of the most energetic people I've ever met. Tawny's hair is dyed jet black like her eyeliner, and Leo has a thick, gray ponytail. I like them already. I want to hear all their stories.

Guitar chords fill the space, and I turn to see who's playing.

My eyes blink in disbelief.

Sitting on a stool in the corner, strumming an acoustic guitar, is Cujo. He doesn't just play. He sings. Well. Very, very well.

His voice is powerful, on par with Chris Stapleton and Teddy Swims.

The magnitude of it fits him, but the smoothness doesn't. At least not what I know of him, which is admittedly not much. Looking around, it appears everyone else knew he had this talent. I'm the only one blown away by it.

This morning has shown me a whole other side to Ivydell. I've been told I arrived in the off season, but I associated the season with the annual arts festival, and assumed it centered on visual artists. Aside from the spirit sisters, whose draw is clearly intangible.

I felt like I knew this place, but my curiosity has been renewed.

Josephine watches Cujo with a contented expression. She's not smiling, but you can just tell the sound of his voice means something more to her.

Jensen comes up behind me and wraps his arms around my waist. He doesn't care who knows we're more than friends, not that it would be easy to keep a secret in Ivydell.

Ironic, given that everyone here seems to be a little secretive by nature. Big secrets are probably easier to hold on to, though. People can read your small secrets anywhere if you give them half a chance.

"Was this worth getting out of bed for?" he asks.

"Definitely worth it." I sip my coffee and lean my head back against his shoulder. "Does this place become a bar at night?"

"People come down here to hang out and have a few drinks sometimes, but no bartender."

"So, I guess that means no band either."

"If you want to go hear a band, I can make that happen."

"A good band?"

"We can hope."

Tawny brings out a tray of fresh-from-the-oven scones. Josephine brings us one.

"Y'all have to share, but she has more in the oven."

"Thanks." I break off a piece and feed it to Jensen.

He pretends he's going to bite my fingers again, the same way he did with the olives during our picnic. I yank my hand away this time, too. And then he pulls it back and kisses it instead.

The scone is delicious. So is he. So is this whole morning.

I turn back to watch Cujo. He's smiling out at Josephine. I glance back to see if she's smiling now, too, but she's not there. Turning my head further, I spot her in the kitchen with Tawny.

He's smiling at Jensen. And Jensen's smiling back. They're friends. An unlikely pair anywhere else, but nothing is all that unlikely here.

The door opens and a man I've never seen stands silhouetted against a swirling sunlit gust of fine desert dirt, glittering like stardust behind him.

"Who's that?" I ask.

Jensen nods his head at the man. "That's Shadow."

"Whoa."

Cujo keeps playing, but his smile is displaced by the furrow of his brow as he watches Shadow enter the coffee shop.

Petra

Like Grandmother Like Granddaughter

Ivy's sweet, but she's stubborn as hell. The way she didn't hesitate to tell me she had no intention of staying away from Jensen—she couldn't be any more like Patty if she tried. But watching her stand there, wrapped in his arms, I still want to go pull them apart.

I care about Jensen, but I can't help but worry about Ivy falling for him. Hell, I more than just care about him; I love him like a son, I guess. As much as I can be maternal. Heaven knows he could've used a better mom, and I'm better than nobody.

I want to protect him from himself.

And her from him, which feels like a betrayal and an obligation at the same time.

I know I hold no power over what's happening between them, and even if I did, it wouldn't undo what happened between Patty and me. If she was here right now, she'd tell me to let it be, that I could no sooner stop those two from falling in love than I could rope the wind.

The wind was her go-to reference for things you couldn't change, and I'm so sure it's what she'd compare her granddaughter and Jensen to that I can hear her saying it, her voice as clear as if she was standing right next to me.

She'd be right, like she always fucking was, but I'd still lie awake and worry about it.

Maybe they'll be good for each other. Or maybe it's just a fling they both need, a right place, right time kind of thing.

But if neither of those things is true, if one or the other of them ends up hurt . . .

Maybe I shouldn't have let Ivy come here. I felt like she deserved to see Ivydell, and I wanted to meet her, but I expected she'd hate it the way her mom did.

I wasn't expecting her to be such a carbon copy of her grandmother instead.

It's hard to think of you as the person she calls Gran. I bet you were a damned good one, Patty. So much change. And so much more on the horizon. I just want to get things right this time. I need the next ending to be happy.

Jensen

Don't be a Lizard

WHEN WE'VE HAD OUR fill of caffeine and catching up, everybody goes their own way. Cujo and I tell Shadow we'll ride back and catch up with him at his place later. He nods, but the way the old man eyes Ivy tells me he's going to be more interested in hearing about what I've been up to with her than talking about why he's back so soon.

He can come back whenever he wants, the same as the rest of us, but he doesn't alter his schedule often. When he says he'll be back on a certain date, it's rare to see him before then.

I follow Ivy to her door, and she laughs. "Are you planning to come in?"

"Unless you tell me you have to work."

She bites her bottom lip, and I already know the answer. "You do, don't you?"

"Yeah, I've got a project on deadline, and I'm afraid if I don't make some progress today, the internet won't be steady for the next few days, and then I'll be in trouble."

"Okay. But tonight, you're mine."

"Am I?"

Backing her against her door, I press my hips into her and pin her arms over her head. "You heard me."

When our lips meet, hers part with no coaxing from me. The taste of her warm tongue makes me want to coax her into letting me come inside. "I could relax you, get your day off to a good stress-free start."

"And then I'll want a nap." She pushes against my chest. "Stop being a bad influence. I only need to work for about five hours. Then we can go to the laundromat together. Nothing says sexy date night like watching someone wash their underwear."

"Do you even know where a laundromat is?"

"Yeah, Josephine and I went last week so I could wash my sheets. But now, I'm almost out of clean clothes."

"You could use my washer and dryer instead. In fact, you could grab your computer and your laundry, and use them while you work. Then you wouldn't have anything to do later other than me."

"Hold on. You have a washer and dryer? What the hell, Jensen?"

"I didn't think about you not having them. Come on. Get your stuff. I'll go to the shop and leave you alone so you can work."

"Okay. Do you have snacks at your place?"

"I have popcorn." The last time I made her fresh popcorn, my mouth stayed busy eating her while she enjoyed both.

"Maybe tonight." She winks.

She tosses some snacks from her pantry and her own detergent on top of her laundry, and puts the basket in the wagon Petra loaned her.

"Why'd you borrow the wagon?"

"I needed it to carry the wood."

"Of course. What wood?"

"The wood to make the sign for Vintage Vibes."

"Oh, you're making the sign, huh?"

"Yeah. I'll probably have Josephine draw the lettering, so it will match your tattoo, but I can paint it. Speaking of—"

"I'll put the ointment on it as soon as we get to my place."

She sets up her computer at my table and lays out her snacks. I show her the washer and dryer inside the shelter I built on the end of the patio to keep dirt from blowing into them. Most of it, anyway.

"They're outside?"

She can't really be shocked. There's no place for them inside.

"It appears that way."

"Okay, smartass. Go take care of that tattoo before you head off to the shop."

"When did you become such a nag?"

"I'm not a nag. But if that shoulder gets infected and your skin starts rotting off like a zombie, I'm not coming anywhere near you."

"See? Now I understand your motive. It's all about your comfort level, not my health."

"Exactly."

I steal another kiss before I force myself to leave her alone.

LESS THAN AN HOUR later, Ivy bursts into the shop, panting and shaking her head. "I need you to come get rid of a huge fucking lizard."

"How do you propose I do that?"

"I don't care. Kick it. Throw rocks at it. Smack it with a shovel! Just get it out of there so I can finish my laundry."

"Tropical girl who's afraid of lizards. How'd you survive?"

"I'm not from the tropics. I'm from the Gulf Coast, and I can assure you our lizards do not look like little pissed off dinosaurs!"

"It's hard to keep them out of there. They like the heat."

"Super interesting fact. Seems like the sort of thing you could've mentioned before I got ambushed by one. Can you run them off long enough for me to finish, please? I'll definitely go to the laundromat next time."

"They won't hurt you, but yes, I will come do a sweep of the area."

"Are you making fun of me?"

"A little. But I'm still going to come to your rescue."

"When the dryer is done, I'm going to text you to come get my clothes out. Or at least to do another *sweep of the area.*"

"Perfect. I'm keeping a list."

"What kind of list?"

"Of all the times I save you from the scary prehistoric lizards."

"So I can repay you with sex?"

"That's what I like about you. You're not just a pretty face."

"Yeah, I've been told I've got a nice ass, too."

"True, but if you bring up other guys commenting on it again, I'll be forced to spank it."

"We've had this conversation. I'm not into punishment play."

"Who said anything about punishment? I just get all worked up thinking about your pretty ass. And it definitely makes me want to play."

I've walked her back against the wall next to the door, and she squirms against me. Intentionally torturing me, I'm pretty sure.

"Jensen. You're supposed to be taking care of the lizard."

I glance down between us at my thickening cock. "He likes your pretty ass, too."

She laughs, but she pushes me away as she does it. "Will you and your lizard please go scare away all the other ones?"

"You promise to show your appreciation later?"

"I don't know. I might be in the mood for popcorn."

"You better be."

I rattle the door and shake the washing machine and dryer a bit. No lizards run out, so I assume they've all vacated, but I stand guard for her while she swaps her clothes from the washing machine to the dryer.

"Text me when you're ready for me to come get your clothes. I'll be at Shadow's."

"He's older than I expected. Like . . . old enough that I don't think he should venture off alone like he does. Or even live alone, really. How old is he?"

"Not sure. Early eighties would be my best guess. But he's in good health. Strong. Still got his wits about him. I'm never going to be the one to tell him he has to give up his independence. I feel sorry for whoever has to when the time comes."

"Does he not have any family?"

"Not as far as I know."

"That's sad."

I wince, knowing I don't have any either. Nobody close enough to feel like it, anyway. My distant relatives are distant in every sense of the word. But I don't want to be thought of as sad. People use that word because it sounds nicer than pathetic, but that's the word they mean.

"If you ask me, he's happier than most."

"I still think everybody should have *someone*. If he really has no one, that's a shame."

"He has Ivydell. These are his people."

"I hope you're right that he's happy."

"I am." I kiss her forehead and linger for a moment to feel the heat of her skin on my lips.

She's kind. So damn kind. As long as you're not a lizard.

Ivy

Best Peformance of the Year
Goes to . . .

I WOMAN UP AND get my own clothes out of the dryer, but I'm anxious the whole time. Afraid to keep my feet on the ground for too long, I shift my weight from one foot to the other repeatedly as I yank my clothes from the dryer and toss them into the basket I set on top of the machine. It must look like I'm standing in a bed of fire ants, doing my awkward hop-stomp dance, but I don't care.

Forcing myself to be brave is hard enough with the memory of that original grimacing lizard in my head, but if another one shows his ugly face before I get out of here, I know I'll scream. If one runs across my foot, I'll piss my pants. And then I'll have to do another load of laundry. We'll be trapped in a loop—me versus the laundry lizards.

But I am not texting Jensen to get my clothes out of the dryer. I was taken by surprise earlier, that's all. It's not like I need protection to step outside. My mom would disown me. Gran would roll over in her grave.

I'm a beach girl. I'm not afraid of lizards, but I'd rather not encounter the Jurassic version again. I'm sorry, but lizards with horns? No, thank you.

He looked so angry, too. At me. Like I'd offended his family. Or infringed on enemy turf, and his boss had sent him to have a little talk with me. Except he would say it like "tawlk."

Jensen can claim that thing was harmless all he wants, but he didn't see the way it glared at me with its dead eyes. The way its nostrils flared, and then its whole body puffed up like the 'roids had just kicked in. That little beast went hulk-mode, and it was preparing to lunge at me and take a bite out of my leg. Because, of course, he hadn't really come to just *tawlk*. They never do.

I shake off the replay. One last scan of the dryer drum to be sure I'm not leaving behind a stray sock, and I'm done. Standing confidently on both feet, I grab the basket and turn to take it inside.

The wind gusts and I jump, causing my clothes to bounce, but thankfully, nothing goes over the side. Great. I'm jumping at the wind now?

Something rustles in the cactus at the edge of the patio and I hop-stomp my way inside, quick-quick-quick, slamming the sliding glass door behind me to keep whatever it was out there where it belongs. On lizard turf.

I'm folding the last of my things when Jensen comes in through the sliding glass door. I knew he was out there, saw him walk up and go to the lizard sanctuary, where he keeps his washer and dryer.

"Wow. You got your clothes out of the dryer all by yourself?"

"Yes. Sorry I had a meltdown earlier. I got over it."

"Good to know you're not afraid of horned toads anymore. I bring one in now and then, let it roam around, give it a snack. Sometimes, they get lost in here, but I don't worry about it. They always come out of their hiding spot when they're ready to go back outside."

"Keep it up and I'll go home."

"All the way back to the beach?"

Wow. Did I just refer to my temporary casita, Sparrow's Song, as home? "You know what home I meant. How's Shadow?"

"He's good. Also, a fan of your ass, in case you were wondering."

"I could've gone my whole life without knowing that. Thanks."

"You done working for the day?"

"I shouldn't be, but yes. The lizard kicked me into high gear for a while, but then my adrenaline crashed. I got a lot done, just should've done a little more."

"You conquered your fear of lizards, and your clothes are clean."

"That's at least half-true."

"I could help you accomplish an orgasm." He's already pulling me up from my chair.

"The most enjoyable accomplishment of all. And they don't even give out awards for it."

His grin tells me I've walked right into a joke. "I think they do, actually. And if you want an award from the adult video industry, I'll happily be your cameraman. I'll vote for you and everything. Otherwise, you'll have to settle for my enjoyment of your pleasure."

"Fine. I'll take the consolation prize."

"First, you'll take that spanking I promised you earlier."

"I'm not sure how much of that I'm in the mood to take."

"Let's find out."

He peels my clothes off like he's working for a tip—gentle efficiency, quickly folding my sweatshirt and my leggings before placing them on his nightstand. I'd have tossed them on the floor, but he's more careful with my things. And despite the way he's about to leave marks on me, I know he'll be careful about that, too.

When he pulls my sports bra over my head, I lift my arms to assist him, and when he drags my panties to my ankles, I step out of them and wait for him to put them with my other clothes, not moving to get on the bed yet.

His eyes drinking in my naked body always makes me wetter than anyone else could without touching me. I try to keep my eyes on his, but mine keep drifting to his right hand. The hand that is about to warm up my ass.

My thighs muscles lengthen and contract as I fight not to rub them together. Standing still is a struggle when I want his skin on mine so badly. He rubs his thumbs over my nipples, and my breath instantly shallows.

"I love the way your body reacts for me. Reveals how needy you are. Do you need me?"

"Yes, Daddy."

His body jolts. He was clearly not prepared for me to go there, not yet. But I love the way his body responds as well. With a nod of his head, he instructs me to get on the bed.

I lie face down, but lift my head to drag a pillow down for my cheek to rest on.

He grabs another pillow and works it under my hipbones, propping my ass up slightly, giving him better access to it and my pussy. His warm hand rubs over the globes of my ass, pausing for a few hard squeezes that make my spine arch.

I'm ready for the sting of his hand, growing frustrated in anticipation of it, in fact. He knows exactly what he's doing to me.

Feral-edged groans roll out with his deep breaths as he continues to knead my flesh.

My hips roll on the pillow, and his self-assured laugh feels inexplicably more like praise than degradation. He's proud of himself for working me into this state so quickly, but he's enthralled with me, too.

His fingertips intentionally graze the seam of my pussy as he massages lower on my ass. If he exerts even the slightest bit more pressure, he'll feel the slickness of my arousal. Damn, the way I want him to feel it. It has me rocking up at a steeper angle, encouraging his fingers to slide farther south.

But he won't give me what I want until he's delivered on his promise.

When his hand finally lifts from my ass, I suck in a sharp breath and hold it through the first few strikes. I exhale, and my breathing takes on a rhythm of its own while the impending burn of his hand's next contact commands all my focus.

After a few more blows, my shoulders rise as I instinctively retreat from the pain. He soothes my skin with the circular motion of his palm. No more squeezing or spanking until I've settled again. When he lands the next slap, I relax into the pillow, my body now adjusted, attuned to the abrupt contact and the stinging sensation that remains . . . the heat that's now warming me from the inside out, rising to meet the warmth on my skin, melting me into his bed.

It would be a daring thing to let him know exactly how pliable and compliant I could be for him right now. But beyond the vulnerability he evokes, there is an undeniable trust. A trust too solid and too deep to make sense between us. So soon, but abiding, regardless.

The plateau of solace wanes, and the discomfort once again escalates with each strike. I draw a deep breath as if I can will my body back into contentment, bring the elevator back down, but my pleasure and pain receptors have already punched a higher floor.

"No more." My voice is labored.

"You sure?"

"Yes."

He spanks one more time, but with less force, more tease than torment. "What was that?"

I smile at him over my shoulder. "Yes, Daddy."

"That's my good girl."

Playing with him is such a perfect escape. I love watching the way raw lust changes a man's features—tightened jaw, harder set brow, hooded eyelids and the searing gaze that escapes them—but when it happens to Jensen, it's like watching an electrical grid power back up after an outage. It fills me with fascination, but it brings with it an assurance of something I don't fully understand, yet know my life is better with than without.

He lies next to me, and his strong hand slides between my legs. His fingers skate through my juices. My eyelids flutter, and we both moan. As much as I love his oral skills, I want him to use his fingers without his tongue this time.

"Is this what you want?"

"Yeah, just your fingers."

"Okay. Relax. I've got you."

I hadn't realized I wasn't relaxed, but my jaw unclenches and my shoulders soften. I roll over, and he grips my inner thigh to pull my leg over his. His thumb claims my clit, and two fingers slide into my pussy.

Within minutes, my core tightens and tingling sparks flow through my limbs, followed by tremors in my quads and glutes. My hips rock feverishly, grinding my pussy against his hand, nearly quashing my impending orgasm because my spastic movements shift his thumb off-target. He recaptures my clit before the sensations are completely lost, his hand chasing the right spot while his eyes read my face and body.

When the climax crests, my inhales become inverted screams, and my fingernails dig into his shoulder. He stills and lets me cling to him until the aftershocks subside and my body falls slack against him.

I attempt to roll back over so he can take me from behind while I lazily starfish and enjoy his dick. At least my legs. He can pin my arms over my head. Behind my back, if he wants. I don't care, but that orgasm depleted my energy. I'm more than willing to be a fuck-doll at this point.

But he rolls onto his back and says, "No. Come here. Ride my cock so I can see your beautiful face and those perfect tits."

There's probably a woman somewhere who could say no to that, but she's not in this room. My thighs would like to launch a protest, but apparently, the rest of me is still feeling compliant.

I straddle him and hold myself open while he positions the tip of his cock at my entrance and watches me slide down it. Fuck, the way he stretches me is perfection. And he looks beautiful lying beneath me, watching my pussy stretch to accommodate his thick dick.

Pressing the fronts of my calves into the mattress for support, I arch my spine, letting my head drop back until the tips of my hair brush over his legs. A small shiver runs through him, and then his hands roam up my torso to palm my breasts.

It takes every ounce of my core strength to bring myself back upright. As soon as I do, his hands drift lower to grip my hips.

He lifts me a few inches and lowers me with a provocative grin. I take the cue and ride him like he wants, freeing his hands to reclaim my tits.

He's quiet, no dirty talk, but his gaze moves over my body like he can't get enough of the sight of me. Visual praise that makes my walls clench around him. His hands glide up and down my waist. I pinch my nipples, prompting his hips to jerk.

When I feel sure I've got him close, I plant my feet on either side of him, steady my palms against his chest, and pump faster on his dick. My quads will throw up the white flag of surrender quick on this shit, but I think I can keep them engaged long enough for him to finish.

His jaw locks, and his quickened breathing morphs into loud animalistic grunts as he fucks up into me.

Success! I collapse onto his chest for a minute before I roll off to let him catch his breath fully without the weight of me on top of him.

I smile up at the ceiling.

"Are you laying over there congratulating yourself for that two minutes of work you put in?"

"I'm writing my acceptance speech."

He laughs, and then he pulls me closer and kisses the top of my head. "Do you think you should win for your tits or your ass?"

"Every category. Are you kidding? I'm sweeping these awards."

"Should we go buy a bottle of champagne to celebrate?"

"And chocolate."

"Burgers on the way?"

"Yes. With bacon."

"You keep talking like that and I'm going to get hard again."

"Bring me a towel, and then you can ply me with bacon, chocolate, and champagne. Who knows where the night might lead?"

He rolls out of bed and walks to the bathroom. I can't take my eyes off him.

Jensen

The Real Stuff

Ivy's head whips to the right when I drive past Hilltop Market, watching through the window as we whiz by my preferred wine store. "You missed the parking lot."

"You said we could get burgers first."

"We have to go this far for burgers?"

"For good ones, yes."

I don't specify how far because I know she's hungry, and I didn't bring her any snacks for the ride. And we're still almost an hour away. Before I came to Ivydell, if anyone had told me I'd be willing to drive an hour and a half for a burger, I'd have told them they had me confused with someone else.

But once you live in Ivydell for a while, you get used to putting in extra effort for things you really want.

We could get burgers from somewhere closer, but I'd regret it.

I try to avoid regret these days.

Her sigh becomes a yawn. The evening sun streams in through the windshield to light flames in her hair. That's how it looks, like it could catch fire at any minute. I reach over and touch the strands next to her face, let a section glide between my fingers. It's soft and warm, just like the rest of her.

"If you play with my hair, I'll fall asleep."

"Always, or just right now?"

"Any time."

"Now I know how to tame you."

The teasing shimmer in her eyes contradicts her sweet smile. "Good luck with that."

But she is sweet just the same, no matter how fierce she tries to sound.

We pass cows, and she says, "Cows!" She does the same when we pass goats and sheep. When we pass bison, she calls them buffaloes, and I can't let it go.

"Those were technically bison."

"That is technically pedantic."

"No, they're a different species."

"Everybody calls those bison buffaloes."

"Then everybody is wrong."

"Hey, you worry about wine. Stay in your lane."

"I didn't realize you were a bison rancher."

She scoffs. "There's a lot you don't know about me."

That's true, but I want to change it. "What's your favorite flower?"

"All of them. I really love sunflowers. Calla lilies. Peonies. Plumeria. And birds of paradise."

"That's a flower?"

"Yeah." She pulls up an image on her phone and turns it toward me.

"That's an aggressive-looking flower."

"They're gorgeous."

"Out of all the flowers you named, I only know what a sunflower looks like."

"I'll show you pictures of all the others while we eat our burgers."

As promised, she shows me examples of all the flowers she mentioned, plus dozens more. She really likes flowers. I hope the desert is in bloom before she leaves.

I eat the third of her burger that she can't finish. She ate all her fries, though. They were easier finger foods while scrolling on her phone to find all the flower pics.

"Do you still want champagne?" I ask.

"And chocolate."

"Right. And chocolate."

"You really should've gotten me flowers to celebrate, too. I mean, how often does a girl win these types of awards?"

"Depends on the girl, I guess. How about if I promise to give you flowers before you head back to the beach?"

"And you have to bring me some the first time you come to visit me there."

My smile is instant. I love thinking about visiting her at the beach. Hell, yeah, I'll take her flowers.

Shane greets us when we walk into Hilltop by lifting a bottle over his head. He's always stocking his shelves or moving things around.

"Hey, Stinger! Hello, Ivy!"

It feels good that he remembers her name.

"Hi, Shane!" she calls back. Because of course she remembers his. She's a names person.

I'm better with faces, but her name is memorable. Everything about her is memorable.

"Can I help you find anything?" Shane asks.

"We've come in search of champagne." I grab a bottle of malbec he recommended before. It's definitely worth buying again. His recs are always on point.

"I can absolutely help with that." Shane rounds a corner, and we follow. "What are you celebrating?"

Ivy and I exchange smiles.

"Life."

He twirls a bottle out of the rack. "I always say the best reason to drink champagne is because you want to. But I like to ask about occasions to help gauge the price point. This is an all-around good choice."

I recognize the label. It's an all-around expensive choice is what it is. But he's not wrong about it being good. And she deserves it.

"Thanks, Shane." My deadpan delivery makes it clear I know he handed me this one to see if I'd balk at the cost in front of Ivy. It's not the occasion he wants to know more about; it's my relationship with her. "We're going to grab some chocolate, too."

"Need any help with that?"

"No. You've been helpful enough."

His good-natured laugh has a twinge of gloat to it. It's all right. I feel like I passed a milestone exam after Ivy quizzed me about all those damn flowers, so a celebration is in order for multiple reasons.

She just wanted to know if I'd been paying attention. She took great joy in making me prove it.

I'm always paying attention to her.

"Let me chill this for you." Shane takes the bottle up front while Ivy and I pick out chocolate. I let her choose since I chose last time.

When we get to the register, Shane presents the chilled champagne to Ivy in an insulated wrap. "The bag's on the house."

"You're too generous," I joke, figuring that bag was probably a freebie from the distributor.

Shane winks, confirming my guess was accurate, but when he says the total for our purchases out loud, Ivy grabs my forearm. "How much is this champagne?"

"You have expensive tastes in chocolate."

She rolls her eyes, knowing the chocolate was not the prime offender. "We can get something cheaper."

"No, we can't." I lift her hand from my arm and kiss her fingers before I pull my wallet from my pocket.

Back at my place, it feels almost disrespectful to pour this champagne into generic wine glasses, but that's all I've got. It's been a long time since I've cared about anything so esoterically tied to my past. The correct stemware left my conscious concern years ago, but tonight, I wish I had crystal flutes.

"Congratulations on your outstanding accomplishments."

She takes the glass I'm offering. "I'd like to thank my supporting cast for allowing me to shine." The rim of her glass clinks against mine.

"Supporting cast, huh?"

"Cheers to my costar?"

"Cheers."

I sit on the bed with my back against the headboard and spread my legs so she can take her place between them. "Get in your spot and tell me more new things about you like the last time we sat here."

"The last time, you were trying to keep my mind off the pain of my scorpion sting."

"Partly. But I wanted to get to know you, too. I still do."

"I want to know more about you, too." She slides into position, and I wrap my arm around her ribcage, hold her back against my chest. "Why'd you come here?"

She not only strikes first; she goes straight for the jugular. Okay. "I was looking for somewhere that felt right when nothing else in my life did."

"Was it right after your parents died?"

"No. After I sold the winery, I went to school. Becoming a mechanic seemed like a good fit. I wanted something that would keep my hands busy, a job I could leave behind when I clocked out. A way to be productive but not be expected to do more than go through the motions."

"How old were you when they died?"

"Twenty-three."

"What happened?"

"Car accident. My dad was driving."

"It must've been awful to lose both your parents so young. I'm sorry you had to go through that."

"Losing them wasn't the hard part."

"You weren't close?"

"My dad loved the winery. Loved being a big shot, mostly. But I'm not sure he really ever loved my mom. And I don't know that either of them actually wanted kids. Or maybe they just weren't prepared to raise one."

"Still, losing them both at once had to have been hard."

This is the fork in the road. The moment where I have to make a choice. If I don't tell her everything now and things work out between us, at what point do I share the rest? How long do I keep holding it back?

I think too long and she moves on with her questions, steering the conversation away from the accident, leaving my losses behind like I've been trying to do since I got here four years ago.

"How long were you a mechanic?"

"I was almost twenty-five when I got certified. Landed a job at a dealership right away, but after two years of school, I lasted less than six months. Just woke up one day and couldn't take it anymore. I didn't need the salary, which made me feel like an asshole. All I knew was that I needed another change. A bigger one.

"So, I packed up my clothes, sold or gave away most everything else, and started driving east. Figured I'd stop when I found a place that felt right. Or when I reached the Atlantic Ocean, whichever came first."

She laughs softly in my arms, takes another sip in silence. I can feel the caution in the sudden tensing of her body. She wants to know more, and if I don't open up now, I might never.

I force the words out. "There was someone else in the car that night."

"You weren't an only child?"

"I was. Her name was Jenna. She managed the tasting room at Stinger Winery. She'd just passed her sommelier exam. A few years older than me. Smart. Ambitious. We'd both tried to convince my dad to open a smaller biodynamic winery and let us run it for him, but he never liked an idea that wasn't his. And he hated that one."

"She was more than a coworker."

"We were engaged. Too young, probably, but nobody could've told us that."

"You were Jensen and Jenna? That's seriously fucking

adorable.”

"Yeah, she always thought so, too. We had big plans. She was leaving Stinger Winery. So was I. We were going to open the biodynamic winery on our own. Cut ties.”

"Did your dad know?”

"He knew she was leaving. She'd given him her resignation with thirty days of notice, which was more than he deserved. I never shared my plans, and he never asked, but I'm sure he assumed I'd follow her. He was angry, but he'd always been angry.”

"Where were they all going together?”

"There was an annual charity gala coming up. All the wineries in the area took turns hosting. It was Stinger Winery's year. It's why Jenna offered to stay for thirty days. They were going to a meeting that she didn't really need to attend, but he insisted, and she didn't want to cause any more conflict. Everybody knows everybody in the industry.”

"Did they make it to the meeting?”

"No. He crossed over into oncoming traffic and hit a truck head-on. They were all dead by the time the ambulances got there.”

"Oh, God, Jensen. I'm so sorry.”

"I don't know what was going on in the car that caused him to do that. But he did it. He killed her. He killed all three of them. There was nobody alive to answer questions, so I'll never know why it happened. But I'll always wonder if they were arguing about me, and he turned around to yell at her. He always wanted to look you in the eye when he had a point to make. Intimidation was his favorite tactic.”

Her tears fall onto my arm. I don't want her to cry. Not about this, not about anything ever, but I'm glad I told her. It's a relief to share this part of my story. But it's unfair to burden her with my tragedy when she's still processing her own grief. Fuck.

There's no good way, no right time to reveal this stuff. No easy path. She deserved to know, though. My history is fucked up. It's not fair to let her walk further into my life blind to it.

She wipes her eyes, tilts her head back, and kisses me softly.

"If you have more questions, you can ask, Ivy. I'll tell you whatever you want to know."

"I'm sure I'll have more soon, but not tonight. But if you want to talk about it some more, please do."

"Not tonight."

"You can talk about her around me, Jensen. Always. I can't imagine how hard it's been to keep her memory bottled up. Not to share your stories that include her. It doesn't have to be a secret you keep locked away. Jenna is always going to be a part of you. And I'll always understand that. I promise."

I play with her hair, but not to make her sleepy. I just need to feel the softness of it.

She blinks away fresh tears. "Do you want to go sit outside and stare at the stars while we drink more champagne, and just listen to the silence together? To just be for a while?"

"More than I've wanted anything in a long goddamned time. But, um, how long do you actually think you can be quiet before something freaks you out and you lose your shit?"

"There's only one way to find out." She shrugs. "Peace only ever lasts for so long. You've got to enjoy it while you can."

"You willing to share that chocolate?"

"Only with you."

Ivy
Here's to Strong Women

IT'S BEEN A FEW days since Jensen told me about Jenna, and keeping my mind on work has been harder than usual. He hasn't mentioned her again, but he seems lighter for having talked about it.

I want to know more, but I won't ask. I'll let him talk when he's ready, but I hope that's soon because I'm so full of questions I could burst.

I'd love to see a picture of him from before that tragic night when he lost so much. Some lives have a defining before and after moment. There's no denying that accident had to have been his. I hope he has pictures of Jenna and him together. Pictures of him growing up.

Would he have kept those things?

There was no one to guide him, to tell him he should keep things like that. That even if he didn't think he wanted them then, he would someday. I have to believe there's a storage unit somewhere with boxes of his life, secure and waiting for him to be ready to reclaim them.

Thinking he might not have any photos of the people and places that shaped him seems like insult to injury to me. I imagine us going through a box of photographs together. Him showing me the vineyard and the house he grew up in. His childhood pets. Maybe he at least has some saved digitally.

My mom would love to take him on a photo journey through my childhood, I'm sure. The awkward teen years, me gardening with Gran, but paying more attention to the ladybugs than the plants, and her attempting to teach me how to paint.

I never had the patience for growing things or for capturing all the nuances that turned brush strokes into art, but I wish I'd known Ivydell was active again before she died.

She and I could've come here together. She would've been so proud to introduce me to her old friends, show me around, and tell me her favorite stories about this place and the people who shaped her.

Maybe Petra feels like company.

As soon as I walk outside, Josephine pulls up next door. She rolls down her window. "Where are you going?"

"To see if Petra's home and if she's in the mood for company. Wanna go?"

"Yeah. I'll unload my stuff and catch up. You care if I ask Myrna if she wants to come, too?"

"No, that's fine." If the four of us hang out together, it seems like we should invite all the women. "What about Tawny?"

"I'll text her. She'll probably want to come."

There are two other women currently in Ivydell, though I'm not sure they're the type who really care for girls' night activities. Maybe they did at some point. "What about Alma and Elma?"

"Never hurts to ask. If the spirits have them occupied, they'll let you know."

What does that mean? Am I supposed to invite them? I guess it's only fair if she's going to reach out to Myrna and Tawny. That's what I get for opening my big mouth. I don't want them to feel excluded, though.

I like the Spirit Sisters, or what I know of them so far, anyway. But I've never been to their casita. They seem like they probably aren't crazy about drop-in guests. From what I understand, most of their visitors are clients who come for readings or channeling sessions. Even their spirit visitors supposedly keep to a schedule.

But they are an integral part of Ivydell. More so than me, that's for sure. I shouldn't be afraid to walk up to their doorstep.

They have two casitas that share the name Whispering Winds. The houses each have a lettered tile mounted near the front door. They live in the one marked A and work in the one with the B. Maybe the spirits stay in B, I think as I walk up to A.

Alma opens the door when I approach. "Hello, sweet Ivy."

"Hi. I hope I'm not disturbing, y'all."

"Oh, no, not at all. Elma is making us some tea. Would you like a cup?"

"Actually, I was wondering if you and Elma might want to go with me to Petra's? Josephine is checking with Myrna and Tawny to see if they want to come."

"Oh, that sounds wonderful. Come in."

Not sure I want to do that, but I don't want to be rude, either, so I step inside their living space. It's dark, but not creepy. Elma has overheard our conversation, and she's already stepping out of her slippers to put on a pair of shoes better suited for walking.

Alma says she needs to freshen up, and then she disappears into the bathroom. I have a feeling this could take a while. Gran never just grabbed her purse and walked out the door without checking her hair and makeup in the mirror, touching up whatever she felt needed it.

Mom is less fussy, probably because she's used to switching gears quickly after so many years of working in the emergency room. She can be ready to go in a flash. I'm like her. I can usually be out the door in under ten minutes, unless it's a special occasion, or if I just woke up.

Josephine texts to say she and Tawny are meeting Petra at the community center, and we should come there instead. Then she calls to say Tawny is bringing a few bottles of wine. She says if I have any, I should bring it.

Okay, so this really is going to be a girls' night. I explain the change of plans to Elma. She loves the idea of everyone gathering at the community center, but informs me she and Alma don't partake of alcohol. She'll bring her teapot.

"While you're getting your teapot packed up, I'll run back to my place and grab a bottle of wine."

"Oh, that sounds fine. You can go on ahead. We'll be there soon."

Is it wrong to leave these old women to make their own way to the community center? It won't be dark for hours. They walk all over Ivydell every day.

I leave, still unsure, but glad to go. Being in their casita made me nervous.

It felt like time slowed down the moment I stepped through their door. I'm happy to assume a brisk pace on the way back to Sparrow's Song. No letter and no spirits.

Tawny says Leo is coming down in a bit to throw burgers on the grill. Apparently, Jensen and Cujo are bringing fish they caught today, and Dice is coming over to help with the cooking.

Nobody thinks twice about the men cooking while the women sit idly inside, sipping wine and chatting. No wonder Gran loved this place. Not that the women don't work around here to keep this place going. Everyone does whatever needs doing. The way it should be.

I need to make sure I do my share. They might not ask me for much since I'm temporary, but I don't want to be treated like a guest.

Jensen comes inside and sets another bottle of wine on the table. It's the malbec he bought on our last trip to Hilltop. He kisses the top of my head before he goes back outside.

Myrna shimmies in her chair. "Ooh, I bet you've got some spicy stories you could share about Stinger."

"No, she does not," Petra says.

"I don't kiss and tell."

Josephine raises her eyebrows and mouths, "But you'll share with me."

Right, like she'd share anything about her and Cujo. I just laugh and shake my head.

"Gran must've loved it when everyone got together here."

Petra nods and smiles. "Oh, she did. Patty loved to sit and gab."

"She was a talker." I refill my glass and top off Tawny's.

Tawny and Josephine say they wish they could've met her. I love them for saying that because it inspires Petra to share stories about her. Hearing Gran introduced to them through these stories introduces her to me, too. I wasn't born yet when she lived here, so this woman is new to me.

This is what I came here for. I sit lower in my chair and listen, watching Petra's features soften and her eyes brighten as she talks about the woman she calls Patty. The woman who became Gran.

The more I hear, the more real it becomes that she truly was an entirely different woman back then. We're all different people at different stages of our lives.

I've always felt like I knew exactly who I was, but I feel like I'm in a becoming stage right now, on my way to being someone else. Outward change doesn't scare me, but I've never been so acutely aware of changes within me.

I was comfortable being who I was before Gran died, but the moment she left this world, something split apart inside me. I've been counting on the grief to cycle the way people say it does, expecting to wake up one day and be on the other side of it and back to myself. Sitting here in this odd place, I realize I won't ever be that woman again. She was changed irreparably. And that's okay. That acceptance arrives so abruptly, I break out in a sweat.

No one else seems to notice, but for a few moments, I feel like I'm standing in the corner, watching us all drinking and laughing. I see myself, but I don't know her. I love her, and I know she's going to be okay, but I don't know how yet. And for the first time since Gran flew, that doesn't scare the shit out of me. I believe it, and that's enough.

Hearing my name brings me back to my chair. "What about me?"

"Pay attention," Josephine teases. "Petra was saying how you don't just look like your grandmother. You *are* your grandmother."

Everyone laughs again, and I join in this time.

"Strong women raise strong women." I lift my glass.

Tawny leads the toast. "To strong women. May we know them. May we be them. May we raise them."

Everyone says, "Cheers!"

Except Josephine, who says, "Amen to that shit!"

"Gran always said all women are strong. Some just—"

"Haven't found their strength yet," Petra finishes the quote.

"I guess she'd been saying that for a long time before she ever said it to me. When I was a teenager, I told her that women who couldn't find their strength were weak by definition."

Petra winces in preparation to hear Gran's response.

"She told me the only time a woman is truly weak is when she steps on the back of another woman to raise herself higher."

Josephine nods. "Your grandma was a fucking queen."

"Yeah, she was."

My phone lights up on the table. It's a text from Mom.

Hope you had a good day. Miss you.

I miss you, too. I'm sitting in the community center drinking wine with all the women here and listening to Petra tell stories about Gran.

I'm glad you're getting to know her.

Me, too.

She means Petra, but I mean both her and Patty before she became Gran. I like them both an awful lot. Every iteration of me will be a better woman for having known them.

Ivydell isn't a place I could live long term, but I'm glad I trusted my gut when it told me to come here.

Alma and Elma stand and say their goodbyes. Tawny yells for Leo to come drive them back to Whispering Winds. They protest, but he says the men all drew straws, and he won, so he gets the honor of driving them home tonight. He's a good guy.

As they walk past, Alma bends down, gives my shoulders a quick squeeze, and whispers in my ear, "I'm so glad you listened to her. Patrice would never have urged you to come here if it weren't the right thing."

Gran never told me to come here. She didn't even tell me Ivydell had been resettled. I smile at Alma to be kind, but . . . ohhhhhh.

Petra

The Test of Time

TONIGHT FELT LIKE OLD times. It's not uncommon for a group of us to spend an evening in the community center, sharing food and stories, but having Ivy be a part of it took me back. Every time I looked over at her, I saw Patty sitting there.

Watching her face light up when she laughed felt like a balm for old wounds. But she worried me for a moment. She recovered and went on as if she'd been fine all along, but I saw it. Something shook her. I hope it wasn't anything I said that upset her.

She's in too deep with Stinger. But I guess I saw that coming. Didn't think it would happen so fast, though.

The next few weeks will be busy in Ivydell. It's harder with fewer people coming back this year. There's never a guarantee who all will return, but most of them keep in touch to let me know their plans. We'll have enough to take care of everything for the festival. It'll take a few meetings, but we'll figure it out. We always have. We just have to band together.

There will be smaller meetings, too. To plan for bigger things.

Tomorrow will come. But tonight was good. I loved hearing more about Ivy's relationship with Patty. Glad to know some of her sayings were passed on to the next generation of McAdams women. She taught her granddaughter well.

I hear her wisdom in my head all the time. Every time I fretted about how I could keep Ivy and Stinger apart, she was in my ear.

You can't stop the wind from blowing, Petra.

My need to control things hasn't left me entirely, but my resistance to change has weakened considerably.

Times change.

The wind still blows.

Ivy

What a Difference a Day Makes

JENSEN ROLLS OVER NEXT to me and his hand lands on my pillow, inches from my face. He's out. I've been looking at my phone for ten minutes, and this is the first time he's moved.

"Hey," I say quietly. "Let's get up and go get some coffee."

He mumbles in his sleep.

I sit up and play with his hair. He groans and rolls his head away, but it's not out of my reach, so I playfully scratch all over his scalp until he opens one eye.

"Coffee shop's open."

"We were there until one in the morning."

"No. That was the community center. The coffee shop was closed until twenty minutes ago. Totally different thing."

"It's in the same place."

"But last night it had wine. This morning, it has coffee. And baked goods. Let's go get some."

"Show me your tits."

I'm naked. One yank and he could see them easily enough.

"Since you asked so nicely."

I tease the sheet back and forth across my chest. He opens his second eye. Rocking the fabric lower, I go slow. So slow.

A grin replaces his grumpy face. "You have a mean streak, you know that?"

"I don't know what you're talking about." I've barely revealed the top swells of my breasts.

He yanks the sheet down and lunges for me. I squeal and squirm, grappling for the hem that I have no chance of retaking from him. Pinning my arms above my head, he kisses his way down my neck and continues downward until his mouth reaches my nipple.

I stop feigning resistance and enjoy the heat of his tongue, the warm suction he's settling into. This is nice. But we just did this six hours ago. And I really need coffee.

"While you're getting comfortable there, I'm getting cranky up here. You better caffeinate me soon."

His messy hair and sleepy eyes are almost irresistible.

"You think this is comfortable?" His erection pokes my thigh. Laughter from me is not the reaction he's seeking, but I can't help it. He's so predictable I felt this move before he made it.

"I'm sore from last night."

"Is that supposed to make me feel bad? Because if I'm being honest, it feels more like an ego stroke." He raises his eyebrows.

"No strokes for you until after I've had coffee."

He releases my wrists, shaking his head. "Mean. Cruel. Vicious. Wicked." His stream of adjectives keeps flowing as he walks to the bathroom.

I can hear him in there grousing in the mirror about it being too early, grumbling about how he wanted to sleep some more.

He's cute when he's cantankerous.

The wind is blowing, but it's warmer than it has been. I hardly need the sweatshirt I pulled over my tank top. Yesterday, a sweat-shirt was barely enough. It's that time of year all over Texas, I guess. Jackets one day, short sleeves the next.

By the time we've had a couple cups of coffee and said good morning half a dozen times, it's warmed up considerably. I pull my sweatshirt off as we walk outside to leave.

"When did you put on a bra?"

"While you were complaining about me to yourself in the mir-ror."

He laughs. "You deserved everything I said about you."

The warm breeze feels amazing, but it reminds me I didn't bring many clothes for warmer weather. When I was packing, I focused on leggings and sweaters, figured I'd buy whatever I needed here as the weather changed. That was before I had a clear vision of my shopping options.

I kiss Jensen goodbye when we reach the shops, and walk the rest of the way back to Sparrow's Song alone. The Spirit Sisters meet me before I make it to my casita, both wearing khakis, similar, but not perfectly matching floral long-sleeved shirts, and their identical purple puffer vests. Their gray wavy hair is loose instead of in the long braids I've gotten used to seeing on them.

They're getting a late start this morning.

"Good morning. I didn't expect to see you two this late in the morning."

"Oh, we've had a busy morning," Alma says.

"Yes," Elma agrees. "The spirits are active early today. Much to be tended to."

"Nothing too troubling, I hope."

"The spirits never bring trouble."

"Only truth."

Okay, that wasn't vague at all. I probably don't want specifics. "Well, that's good. Enjoy your walk."

"Clear skies today," Alma says.

Elma smiles. "Enjoy your journey. It's going to be a good one."

That was dramatic. I'm less than a hundred feet from my front door. Not much of a journey left. She probably meant it in a more general sense. Those two are difficult to translate sometimes.

Josephine walks to her car with a duffel bag slung over her shoulder.

"Hey! Where are you going? It's Tuesday."

"Special request. I wouldn't normally make the trip for just one session, but this is a VIP client. What are you doing today?"

"I need to go clothes shopping. Any suggestions for where I should do that?"

"Uh, yeah. Albuquerque. Get in. You can take my car and shop while I work, and then we'll go to dinner and have a sleepover at my place. It'll be fun. We'll get an early start out tomorrow. You'll be back here, ready to work by mid-morning."

"I only intended to shop for a few hours and work the rest of the day. But that is such an appealing offer."

"It's still open."

"I don't have a bag packed. I assume you're on a schedule."

"You've got twenty minutes."

That's ten more than I need. "Okay!"

I let Jensen know my change in plans.

> *Your raincheck sex just got delayed by a day. I'm going to Albuquerque to shop.*

> *With Josephine, I assume.*

> *Yep. She's your cockblock.*

> *Be safe.*

The weight of that isn't lost on me. He's lost more than anyone I know because of a car that didn't stay safe.

> *We will. See you tomorrow.*

My fingers hover over the screen. It seems like I should sign off with more, but there's not a universal word or phrase for what I feel for him. This is another in-between aspect of my life with an uncertain future. I don't know where we're headed. It doesn't feel safe. But I don't want to shy away from it.

I zip up my bag, turn off the lights, and find Josephine already sitting behind the wheel with the air-conditioner blowing her curls. She turns down her music and stops singing when I get in. "Did you let Stinger know I'm stealing you?"

"Totally outed you as a cockblock."

"He'll just want you that much more when I bring you back. He should thank me in advance for the wild sex you'll be having tomorrow night."

"Definitely not passing that along. I have no way of knowing what I'll be in the mood for tomorrow night."

"Pretty sure you'll be in the mood to fuck your hot boyfriend."

My body shudders. "Whoa. Easy on the labels."

"Aw, denial. That's cute."

She drives for about an hour before pulling into the parking lot of a tiny taco stand. It's not a chain fast-food place. We eat at a sun-faded picnic table and wash it down with homemade aguas frescas. These tacos are my new love language.

When we get back on the road, I take my chances with a personal question. We're not in Ivydell anymore, so I figure it's worth a shot. "Why Albuquerque?"

"It's where I'm from."

"You never wanted to leave?"

"I leave sometimes. That's how I met you."

"Right. But aren't you just going from one desert to another? Nothing else ever called to you?"

"So many other things did." She runs a hand through her curls. "Look up Ink Trials, season four."

I search it on my phone, knowing because she followed the name with a season it's going to be a TV Show. "Holy shit. You were on a reality show?"

"Not just on it. I won. Instead of competing in the same studio, we all did two-week internships at famous shops, and all the owners rated us at the end of each term. Every time we made it through another round, we switched shops. The goal was to survive them all, but that meant being able to navigate all the personalities and management styles of the owners, on top of meeting the clients' expectations, and being the best artist. We had no idea what was going on in the other shops, how our competitors were doing, until the end of the two weeks when it was time to move."

"You had to move every two weeks? For how many weeks?"

"Twelve. From Houston to Detroit to Chicago to New York to Miami to Los Angeles."

"You remember the order of all your moves without even thinking about it?"

"I'll never forget it."

"Was there any downtime in between?"

"We usually had Sundays to ourselves, if our flights stayed on schedule. Every other Friday, there was a video conference where we all heard everyone's ratings and comments. That's how we found out if we were headed home or to our next shop. Either way, we were all on planes the next morning. If we were going to a new shop, we started there on Monday."

"That's intense."

"I collapsed in my hotel room in LA after the final episode. It wasn't good. Three months of insane hours and pressure, being screamed at, criticized excessively because nice doesn't boost ratings, and all the infighting between the competitors . . . it took a toll."

"How could you fight? Y'all weren't even in the same location."

"We had to participate in an online forum that was all filmed. All the comments, our insecurities and worst moments on full display. Everyone was exhausted, so it took very little to trigger anyone's temper. Not to mention, we didn't get to know each other. There was no camaraderie. Only competition. And then, of course, the footage was all edited before the episode aired. Never to show us in the best light."

"Did you plan to stay in Albuquerque when you came back?"

"I didn't move home right away. One of the artists I worked with in Miami was starting his own shop in Las Vegas. It was never mentioned on-air, but we all knew it was happening. He hired me as soon as the results were announced. He's a huge name in the business, so clients were guaranteed, which was good for me. Being able to advertise that he had the winner of Ink Trials on staff was good for him."

"It didn't work out, I take it."

"Not because of him. He was great. I was still fucked up, barely functioning, but I didn't know how bad it was yet. I thought I could shake it off and keep going."

"You needed time to recover from all the stress."

"Honestly, I wasn't really in a good place when the show started, but after it . . . yeah, I was not okay."

"He wouldn't let you come back once you felt ready?"

She smiles. "He's the VIP client I'm making this trip for. I run the shop in Albuquerque like it's mine, and he runs Vegas, but we're partners. He's done more for me than anybody. Ever."

All the questions I've had about her and Cujo multiply. "Were you ever a couple?"

"No. It was never like that. He might've saved my life, though."

"I'm sorry for all the hard stuff you had to go through. But what you've achieved is amazing. The courage to follow your own unconventional path is impressive."

"I wasn't brave. My talent was just all I had. Nothing else fit. My family never missed an opportunity to let me know how stupid I was to think I could make a living as a tattoo artist. They've come around, but some scars don't heal."

"Yeah, I could see how they wouldn't."

We ride in silence for a while, but when she reaches to turn the music back up, I ask a bolder question. "You want to talk about you and Cujo?"

"I think I've shared all I need to for now."

"Fair enough."

Before she adjusts the volume, she says, "I don't know any details, but apparently, Stinger used to talk to Cujo a lot about his past. He opens up when they're fishing or lifting weights together. But lately, all he talks about is you."

That shouldn't light sparklers in my stomach the way it does. We're not teenagers. But I'm dying to know everything he's said. I know Josephine is telling the truth when she says she doesn't know any details. I can't see Cujo betraying Jensen's confidence. Or anyone else's.

I've never been to Albuquerque. I excitedly take in every detail as we come into town. Josephine's condo is downtown and right around the corner from her shop. It's a studio loft, but it's spacious. Gorgeous.

She has a little time before she has to meet with her VIP, so she walks me around the area a bit to help me get my bearings. I don't really need her car because there are several boutiques that catch my eye. They're probably more expensive than stores I could find if I drive a little farther out, but I'm smitten with the walkable shopping in her neighborhood. Such a stark contrast to her life in Ivydell.

I tell her I'm good when she offers me her car keys. "All I need is a key to get back into your condo when I'm done. I think I'll be able to find everything I need within walking distance."

"The shops around here are all going to be pricey."

"That's okay. I haven't splurged on myself in a while."

She wishes me luck, hands over her access card, and then she leaves me to spoil myself.

Once I get started, I have no trouble at all finding more than I need. I pick out a few sundresses that aren't my usual style, but I love them on the hanger. I send Mom pics of me in each one to be sure I'm not just enamored because I'm in a new place. She'll be honest.

Mom's enthusiastic approval squeezes my heart a little. It's like a virtual hug, and it makes me long to hug her for real. By the time she replies, I'm almost ready to buy them, regardless, but her endorsement seals the deal.

Back in Josephine's condo, I go through all my bags and tell myself I didn't spend too much. These things were all worth it. The only item I second-guess is a headband, but that twenty bucks didn't make a grand difference. I'm not sure I'll really wear it, but the saleswoman said all the right things to make me believe I would when I was contemplating it while twirling in one of my new sundresses.

I nap on Josephine's bed until she calls to say she's done in the shop and tells me where to meet her for dinner and drinks. It's just across the street. Super cute pub, but I'm disappointed I don't get to meet her business partner. He apparently has a partner of the non-business variety in town, too, and they already had plans together.

It's funny to see her in this setting. She looks like she belongs here, but the moment I met her in Ivydell, I thought she belonged there, too. She's adaptable, but also smart enough to know what she needs to make her life work.

Finding her balance may have come at a cost, but she's thriving on her own terms. Her choices would seem bizarre to some people, including the person I was three weeks ago. The person I am right now admires the hell out of her.

She's not the type of friend who wants to ooh and ahh over my purchases. All she wants to know is if I'm happy with them. Part of me wants to pull them all out of the bags and show off each piece, but she'd shut me down. Knowing I'm satisfied is where her concern ends. And that's okay.

Mom will put up with the pictorial fashion show I'm going to send her tomorrow.

Jensen might indulge me, though he'll be much more interested in how easily the outfits come off. That's okay, too.

We get on the road early to head back to Ivydell. We've been gone less than twenty-four hours, but it feels longer. Stopping at the same taco stand feels obligatory, like it's our thing, a tradition, even though we've only done it once.

I wonder if we'll ever do it again after today. Maybe I'll introduce someone else to it someday. I'll think of Josephine if I do.

"Hey, before I forget, will you help me with the sign for Jensen's casita? I need you to do the lettering to match the way you did it on his tattoo."

"Yeah. Of course."

The last hour of the ride goes by in a flash.

Petra and Dice are standing in front of Myrna's casita, talking with concerned looks on their faces. When we get out of Josephine's car, they all stand taller and force smiles as they wave to us. Stiff. Fake.

"Is it just me?" I ask.

"Uh-uh. Something's up. I've never seen the three of them standing around, shooting the shit together. Dice only buddies up with the guys. He's nice enough, but he doesn't just randomly hang out with Petra or Myrna."

Jensen is at my door five minutes later. His welcome home kiss is warm, but his body is tense.

"Did something happen here while I was gone?"

"You were only gone for a day."

"I know. But it seems like there's a weird tension in the air."

"Oh, no. Are the spooky sisters rubbing off on you?"

"Don't patronize me like that. What's going on?"

"Nothing, as far as I know."

His words are rushed and he won't look me in the eye. He's a direct eye contact guy.

"Why are you being weird?"

"If I had to guess, I'd say sexual frustration." His firm hands grab my hips, but instead of pulling me to him like he usually does, he steps forward to bring his body to mine.

"How about a fashion show? I can model all my new clothes for you."

"Yes. You put them on, and I'll take them off." Okay, maybe he's not acting weird after all.

Jensen

Intermission and Encores

I think Ivy bought out an entire boutique while she was in Albuquerque. She looks amazing in every outfit, especially the sundresses. But she looks best in between outfits when she lets me undress her.

Taking off her clothes could never get old, but my dick is throbbing.

She still has one more bag to go, but I can't wait. "Intermission."

I pull her onto the bed with me and kiss her before she can argue. Her body relaxes as I deepen the kiss. She maneuvers her limbs to assist as I remove her bra and panties. When I slide my hand between her legs, she moans into my mouth, and I know she wants this intermission as much as I do.

Her pussy is soaked. My fingers probe her until she circles her hips, thrusting to force my fingers deeper. I bring my hand to her mouth and press my fingers between her lips. She sucks them into her mouth and lets me slide them in and out until she's cleaned her arousal from my skin, her tongue dancing over them when I hold them still.

I debate whether I want to replace my fingers with my dick, knowing I won't last long in her hot, wet mouth. She said she was sore yesterday. Maybe she'd rather I fuck her mouth.

"You still sore?"

She shakes her head no, her eyes looking like glass as she stares up at me. I need to feel my dick in her mouth, anyway. At least for a little while. Neither one of us has had enough sleep lately, but I want to stay up all night with her.

When my fingers leave her mouth, she licks her lips. My dick jumps. I can't get it out of my pants fast enough. She doesn't need any prompting. She knows exactly what I want. I lie flat on my back, and she crawls between my legs, dragging her silky hair across my thigh.

Fuck. I could come from that alone.

She licks up the shaft and swirls her tongue around the perimeter of the tip, circling closer to the center. I love when she does this. Her eyes shine up at me when she cleans the pre-cum, tastes me like she's savoring it.

As much as I enjoy what she's doing, I suddenly need to be deep inside her pussy, feeling her tight walls constricting around me.

I pull her up and flip her onto her back. Her legs spread for me as soon as I'm positioned over her. "I love how easily you give up this sweet pussy."

"Only for you, Daddy." She drags her fingernails up my back. Goosebumps cover my shoulders and spread down my arms.

"Mmmm, you could make a good man do bad things."

"Nothing you do to me is bad."

"I said a good man." I kiss her neck, bite at the base as I sink into her juicy snatch.

She gasps while I advance, stretching her without pausing. Her legs spread wider, and then she draws one in to wrap around my lower back. "You are a good man."

"Who told you that?"

"I don't need to be told." Her hips circle again, her ass grinding against my balls.

I'm not sure if I'm a good man, but she is better than good. And I want her woven into every part of my life. All our fears and desperation and triumphs intricately stitched together like a tapestry. It's too soon to say things like that out loud. Too soon to be thinking about them, but my brain switches to autopilot when her clothes come off. Half the time when her clothes are on, I'm having dangerous thoughts about her, too.

Her nipple contracts between my fingers, and I squeeze incrementally harder until she whimpers. The way her body responds when I'm rough with her sends me so close to the edge. Her warm juices gush around my cock to flood the sheet beneath us.

And then she moans softly as I release her nipple. Her expression radiates ecstasy. She lets go for me, gets lost in the pleasure, trusts me to find her limits.

The pressure of her heel digging into my ass, guiding me back into her as soon I pull my hips is more erotic than it has a right to be. She relinquishes so much control, but she still lets me know what she wants.

I give her every inch again, groaning as her tightness pulls me deeper.

"You take my dick so well."

"I love the way you fuck me."

Sliding my fingers around her opening at the base of my dick, I coat them good with her slickness, dragging it down to rim her asshole. It cinches tighter as I tease around it. When I push a finger inside, her fingernails carve half-moons into my shoulders. I wedge a second finger in to the second knuckle and she draws a measured breath as her nails engrave deeper indentions in my skin.

My hips rock forward and back, sawing my cock faster and faster into her. I wiggle my fingers to ream her reluctant hole, and she releases a clipped shriek as they slip past her tight protective ring of muscle. Her body grants me access like I've uttered a secret password, enabling my fingers to fuck her ass with the same cadence as my cock plunging into her pussy. Her body accommodates my hunger so exquisitely.

When her eyelids flutter, my dam bursts. I fill her in every way I can, using her until I'm completely spent. I want to feel the bliss of having my cock buried in her perfect ass, but I won't push her to give me anything more than she has tonight. She's tired, and I'm not sure how long it would take me to rise to the occasion again, anyway.

I indulged in more self-love this afternoon before she got back than I'd be comfortable admitting. I couldn't get her out of my head.

"Let's shower together, and then I'll lick your pussy until you come as many times as you want. Until you fall asleep with my mouth worshipping your swollen clit."

"You might have to carry me to the bathroom."

I lift my arm weakly and let it fall limp back onto the mattress. "Oh, shit. We might both have to crawl."

Her husky, drowsy laughter is the sweetest sound I've ever heard. I'd carry her in broken arms to hear that.

"Come here, beautiful."

Ivy
Whistle While You Work

I LOG ON EARLY Thursday morning, intent on making up for my terrible work performance so far this week. I mean, I've performed well in some ways. Jensen would probably give me an excellent performance review, but I've been an awful employee. I text Zara to check in.

> Hey, is anybody complaining about me?

> You still work here?

> Haha. As far as I know.

> You're fine. How's it going in the wilderness?

> All good on the western front.

> Are you day drinking at eight in the morning?

> Only water.

> Are you sure the water's safe to drink?

I haven't started glowing yet.

Do you like it there?

Weirdly, I do. It's hard to explain.

Not gonna lie, I kind of want to see the place.

Come visit!

Now I know you're drunk.

Think about it.

Do some work for a change.

It's easy to focus on work today. My mind doesn't wander the way it's been doing so often lately. But when I break to make myself some lunch, I can't stop wondering what Jensen says about me to Cujo.

I haven't really talked about him to anyone. There isn't anyone to have those types of conversations with. I've let most of my friendships fade. I'm closer to Zara now than any of the friends I used to spend so much time with. My work friend has become my closest friend. That's not a bad thing. Zara's great. But it's weird how I had such a solid group of friends for so long, and then we just drifted apart.

Some of them moved, and we didn't keep in touch like we said we would. Some have gotten married. A few had babies. Our lives look so different now. We don't fit in each other's worlds anymore. Or maybe we could, but it would take so much more effort than it used to.

Is it me? Am I selfish? That's what my last serious boyfriend said. As he was packing up his stuff to move out of my apartment. No, fuck him. He was a man-baby who wanted someone to take care of him. Cook his meals and wash his clothes. Ugh. The sex wasn't even great. How he ended up living with me remains a mystery.

The guy before him said he thought I lacked the emotional maturity to maintain a relationship. I wasn't too immature; I just didn't trust him. For good reasons. Based on verifiable incidents. He got caught, but I got shamed. All the twisted shit he said at the end went in one ear and out the other. I shunned his attempt to gaslight me.

But his words still made me question myself after he was gone. There was never any doubt I was done with him, but was I capable of making things last with anyone? I'm still not sure. It's never just one person who's at fault, right?

Jensen seems too good to be true. He has to have faults. They could be huge. What would he be like if we weren't here in this isolated place? Out there in the real world, who is he?

He's used to taking care of himself. I know that much. And I think he was raised to be accountable for his actions. If anything, he might shoulder blame that isn't even his to carry. He's definitely capable of love. Or he was at one point.

How much did losing her take? He has questions that will never be answered. What does that do to someone?

When I realize I've been staring at my computer screen for the better part of an hour, I know it's time to call it a day. I meant to put in a few more hours, but I gave more today than I have all week. The sun is still shining, and I need to feel it on my face.

Petra is helping Myrna unload flats of flowers from the back of her SUV. Marigolds.

"Need any help?"

"Sure!" Myrna yells.

"Where are these going?" I wonder why she didn't get a variety. So many marigolds.

"In the planters up front," Petra says. "They'll spread quick. Be nice and thick by the festival."

Myrna sets another flat in the wagon. It's the last one that will fit. This is definitely going to take several trips. I think she should've unloaded them upfront, but I don't question her method aloud. She hands me a flat to carry. "They'll be a blanket of orange by then."

I'd noticed the large rectangular planters flanking the gate. At first, I thought they were water troughs. Then I realized there were no animals in Ivydell to use them, and I sort of forgot they were there. They became part of the scenery.

"These will grow here?"

"Not a lot will," Myrna says. "But marigolds are tough."

"Gran always planted them with her tomatoes. She said they kept worms away."

"I taught her that." Petra beams. "They attract bees, too. Good for pollination."

"Yeah, see, that's how I think of marigolds, like functional flowers. I never thought they were all that pretty, but seeing so many of them together like this, they are pretty."

"These simple little flowers can be beautiful if you give them what they need." Myrna closes her lift gate and we head for the planters.

"Did you get soil?" I didn't see any bags in Myrna's cargo space.

Petra nods. "Jensen got a truckload earlier. He's already filled the planters."

Now I know what he's been doing all day. That's a good-guy thing to do, right? It's not fair to keep score, to rate his good deeds like a punch card.

Do ten good-guy things, get a free blowjob!

I smile, knowing I'd reward him before the tenth hole punch. A quick laugh erupts before I can choke it back.

Myrna's sleek platinum hair swings as her head snaps in my direction. "Oh, if the mention of his name instantly calls up something that makes you that happy, I want to know all the juicy details."

"No details," Petra says.

This is absolutely not the right crowd for my hole-punch joke.

"You and I need a private wine or coffee date soon." Myrna cuts her eyes at Petra. "Without Mother Superior around to censor us."

Our resident silversmith isn't wearing boots for this job, not rubber or red snakeskin. Her footwear choice of the day is a pair of silver, glittery Crocs. They're more practical for planting flowers, but Myrna is short even in her heeled snakeskin ankle boots. Without them, she's tiny. She's wearing plain black leggings and a long-sleeved black tee with her logo emblazoned in silver foil on the front. The curlicues look the same as her scrolled silver jewelry. And the naked woman on all fours, backed up to a standing bear, is just as unmistakable.

I bet she was the talk of the garden center. At least her shirt doesn't include the name of her business, Wild Love, beneath the logo like her back windshield does. She told me before she's proud of her logo, but I guess I didn't grasp the depth of her pride because it takes brass balls to wear that in public.

Silver balls, technically. Bear balls. Bare bear balls. Okay, it would be weirder if he were wearing pants. That might be the only thing that could make it weirder.

Good for her, being her authentic self, though.

Petra and I get started putting the marigolds in the dirt while Myrna turns the wagon back to grab another load. Her sparkly Crocs catch the sun as she goes. From a distance, you'd never imagine what a big personality that little body held.

"Do you think we'll have enough to fill these?" Now that I'm standing right in front of them, the planters look much bigger.

"Myrna has never bought too little of anything in her life. I'm sure we'll all be taking marigolds home."

"Perfect. I can put them in little pots at the base of my sign. If there's enough, I'll put some by Jensen's new sign, too."

"Why does he need a sign? His casita doesn't have a name."

"It does now. I named it. Vintage Vibes. Josephine is helping me with the sign. It will be something to remember me by in Ivydell after I'm gone."

Her eyes cloud, and her gaze quickly drops to the marigold she's packing dirt around. "That's nice."

Her tone doesn't match her words. I hadn't thought about her being sad when I have to leave, but I'm a connection to someone she loved and lost. She lost Gran long before I did. She had to lose her twice.

"Yeah, he wasn't all that into the idea at first. I had to convince him to let me name it."

"You can stop there."

"I was going to."

She looks up and smiles. I don't think she really hates the idea of Jensen and me being together. She's just protective of her people. Gran was like that, too. For all their differences, I see more and more similarities between them every day.

I wonder if she and Gran would've lasted if they'd met somewhere other than here.

The orange flower in my hand is going to be more than a functional plant to me after my experience here is over. It's going to be a key to the memory of planting these. To the pots under our signs if we have extras. I hope Myrna overbought.

"How do you water these?"

"Jensen connects several hoses to reach out here from his shop. He takes care of watering them."

"He waters the flowers?" My voice sounds like I'm about to faint. I'm not, but damn. That's a good-guy thing for sure.

"Oh, Jesus. It's not an act worthy of the fucking Nobel Peace Prize. Get a hold of yourself."

There's a certain charm to her roughness. I like it. A lot.

"If you were giving superlatives to the residents of Ivydell, which award would you give Jensen?"

"None. I wouldn't feed his ego."

"He doesn't have a big ego."

"Because I don't go around telling him he's a god for doing simple shit, like watering a plant."

"I don't think it would hurt him to hear he does a good job. I'm not sure he heard it much growing up."

She stops and stares at me. "He's a pretty private person. I have to assume you surmised that on your own."

"He's opened up a little. I may have read between the lines."

"I'm not saying you got it wrong, but I'm not sure how much praise he would put up with." She rolls her eyes before she adds, "From anyone aside from you, I mean. I'm sure he can't get enough of you telling him how pretty he is."

"I have never said that to him." I blow a dead leaf off a marigold as I lift it from the ground. "But, goddess, he is beautiful."

"Pant less. Plant more." Her tone is still grouchy, but a grin quirks at the corners of her mouth. "Did you pick that up from your grandmother? Saying goddess instead of god?"

"Yeah. She never said god. Always goddess. I think I mimicked all her sayings from the time I could talk."

"She had some good ones."

"So many. She was a wise woman."

"Yep."

I sink my fingers into the warm, damp soil. Jensen obviously watered it through when he filled the planters. It feels good on my skin, makes me glad we're not wearing gloves.

Myrna heads back our way. I hear her before I look up to see her head bobbing from side-to-side. She's whistling a melody. What song is that?

"Is she whistling 'Sexual Healing'?"

"Don't acknowledge it. You'll only encourage her."

Jensen

Like a Freight Train

CUJO RIDES UP AS I'm thinking about him. He does that a lot. It's almost as eerie as the spooky sisters. I wait for him to shut his bike off so he can hear me. "Hey, you feel like lifting? It's been a while. I'm afraid I'm getting soft."

His big laugh rolls out almost as loud as his straight pipes. "You do too much manual labor for your muscles to get soft. Your head might be getting soft, thanks to that woman whose bed you can't stay out of."

"We spend as much time in my bed as we do hers."

"Oh, well, that changes everything." He shakes his head like reasoning with me is a lost cause.

To be fair, where Ivy's concerned, it might be. Not that anyone's standing in our way, but I wouldn't hesitate to knock them back if they tried. Even Petra has thrown up her hands and is standing down. For the most part.

I spot for Cujo's bench press. I'd do it anyway, but right now, I'm afraid he's got too much weight on the bar. I know better than to voice my concern, so I silently step my right foot forward and ready myself to assist if he fails. He makes ten reps look easy, and I help him rerack.

"You been lifting without me?"

"No, man. I wouldn't lift without a spotter." He vacates the bench.

"Liar." I swap the weights and lie down. I'm the only one of us who prefers a spotter. It was drilled into me at a young age not to lift without one. I had good coaches. Guess I had to get lucky somewhere.

Cujo clears his throat. "I think you could put a little more weight on that bar."

"And I think you could've put a little less on it."

"Okay."

I change the subject. "Seems like Ivy and Josephine had fun on their trip."

"Yeah, Jojo said it was good."

Huh, that nickname is new. I don't comment on it. "Ivy's apparently a shopper."

"You couldn't tell that by looking at her when you met?"

"For a while, I thought all she owned was leggings and sweaters."

"Yeah, but you probably never saw her in the same one twice."

Now that he mentions it, she was here for over two weeks before she needed to do laundry. I tell him about her lizard encounter.

"That's another thing you should've seen coming."

"I didn't mind."

"Of course you didn't. You don't mind a damn thing about her at this point."

At this point. Does she have any traits that will bother me at some point? It's probably to be expected we'd eventually somehow annoy the hell out of each other. I don't think I'd stay annoyed long, though. But that's not realistic. We'll definitely piss each other off.

We might hurt each other.

I might love her.

She might disappear.

A familiar burn fills my stomach. Haven't felt this in a long time—until a few days ago. Thought I'd gotten ahead of it for good. I tell myself to stop making it out to be more than it is. It's not the same as before. This is just new relationship stuff. Normal. Same as everybody else feels. Been a long time for me, that's all.

We switch places again so he can do another set.

"What does Josephine do that bothers you?"

"Nothing. We don't spend too much time together. That's the secret. Spend as little time together as possible."

"Right. That's how she went from Josephine to *Jojo* since the last time we hung out."

He shoves the bar up from his chest again, but he almost needed me on that one. "You know, just because you're getting your dick wet on the regular doesn't make you ten feet tall."

"Her belief that I'm a good man doesn't make me that, either."

Fuck. The burn's not normal. Not the same as everybody else. It's all mine. And I'm not ahead anymore. I didn't know it was gaining on me, but it's not close. It's here.

"Ah, hell, keep up the front for a while longer."

He laughs, but he doesn't get it. I'm not good. I was for a while, but I'm not anymore. I'm going to lose it, and I'm going to fuck this up. She's going to get fucked up in the process. I can't ruin her life. She deserves so much more than I can give. And I don't deserve half of what I'd take from her.

"Let her keep seeing your sorry ass as a good guy. What's it going to hurt? Maybe if she says it enough, it'll start to feel true to you, too."

"No, I see things as they are. People tell themselves whatever they need to believe, I guess. The fairytale is always better than reality."

"Oh, goddamn, Stinger. You thinking about falling back into some self-loathing now? You gonna try to hate yourself enough again so you can fuck it up and prove her wrong? I thought you were past all that self-destructive shit."

So did I. Goddammit, so did I.

I bite down on the inside of my cheek until I taste blood. How can it still fucking blindside me like this? Why now?

"Why don't you put a little more weight on that bar for me?" I grip it tighter to hide the shaking that's building in my muscles from an entirely different kind of weight.

"I ought to put enough on it to pin your scrawny ass to this bench until you get this pity party bullshit out of your system."

"Your call, I guess."

I should be stronger than this by now. I was stronger. I was fine. And now, this shit's gonna happen all over again? And take Ivy down, too? No. No fucking way.

He stands over me like a mountain. "Really? I see those gears turning in your head. This is the choice you're going to make?"

Like I have a choice. I didn't feel this shit coming for me again. But I know waiting it out doesn't work. If I sit with it, it'll consume me. I got lucky enough to outrun it once. Maybe it's time to head east again. This was always meant to be a temporary stop, anyway.

Cujo rips the bar out of my hands and slams it back onto the rack.

"Get up."

"You wanna try to beat it out of me? Is that what we're doing?"

I stand, and he steps in front of me. "Go ahead, man."

His hand flies up, but instead of punching me, he yanks me forward until our foreheads bang together and holds me there, staring a hole into my soul. "Not on my watch, motherfucker. You will not destroy yourself."

My body trembles uncontrollably. It's a freight train, and I can't get out of the way. All I can do is stand here and wait for it to hit.

"Fuuuuuuuuuuucckkkk!"

Ivy

Granting Yourself
Permission

I FINISH PAINTING JENSEN'S sign and decide to refresh mine while I'm at it. It doesn't occur to me until I'm done that maybe I should've asked for permission before I altered mine. It feels so natural to call it mine, but it's not.

What's done is done.

It had to be done, really. The pots I bought for the extra marigolds are bright and bold. The faded sign would've looked even more shabby next to them.

Maybe I could freshen up all the signs. That's a way I could contribute to help make things look nice for the festival, and leave a small remembrance that I was here. That I was a part of Ivydell for a brief while.

While Jensen's sign dries, I walk over to Petra's casita to confirm it's okay if I repaint everyone's. She's gathering herbs from her aging greenhouse. The plastic panels are yellowed from the sun.

I crack the door. "Can I come in?"

"Get in here. I could use an extra set of hands."

The smell is intoxicating. Herbal scents have always been my favorite, and with this many of them combined, I could sit out here for hours. "What do you need me to do?"

She hands me a small wooden bowl. "Pick some spearmint leaves for me."

"Sure." I stand across from her at a table of herbs that I'm positive is all mint, but they're not all the same.

"Which one is the spearmint?"

"Brighter green with the larger, more textured leaves. Peppermint is smoother and darker green. Purple stems."

"Ah, okay." I pluck a bright green leaf and give it a sniff before I put it in the bowl, just to be sure. Yep, that's definitely spearmint.

"Something on your mind?"

"I was wondering if it would be okay if I repainted all the signs for the casitas. To freshen them up before the festival."

"No, that's not necessary."

"But can I do it just because I want to?"

She scowls like I'm trying her patience. I don't mean to be, but I expected her to say yes. Figured asking was a formality. Never imagined she'd say no. We're doing other things to make the place visually appealing. Why not update the signs?

"It's just that the signs—"

"I might have already updated mine," I blurt, fearing she's about to reveal something sentimental and meaningful that will make me feel ten times worse about changing mine without her blessing.

She sighs, but laughter chases it. "You know what? I think it's the perfect tribute to her."

"Oh, shit. Was Gran the last person who painted them?"

"She was. And I think she'd absolutely love to have her granddaughter freshen them up. Go for it."

"I'd like to leave yours alone if that's okay with you." It feels like the best way to honor both her and Gran.

"I think her ghost would kick my ass if I let you do that. The brush has been passed. You are now the official sign painter of Ivydell."

"Perfect. I'll come back around in another thirty years when they're due for their next makeover."

A curtain of sorrow passes over her face. She tries to pretend nothing is wrong, tells me that filling the bowl with spearmint leaves is the cost of my painting permit.

Dammit. She's in her seventies, and I just told her I'd see her again in thirty years. Could I commit any more blunders today?

As I continue to pick the mint leaves, the release of the oils perfumes the air between us. It's a mood lifter, and before long, Petra's face is free of any sadness. And I feel slightly less guilty for being an oblivious asshole.

I can't stop bringing my hand to my face as I walk back to Sparrow's Song. Fresh mint smells so amazing. I snagged a few peppermint leaves to munch on before I left the greenhouse. I wanted to smell them as much as I wanted to taste them.

Josephine's car is gone when I get back. She never stays put for long. I repaint her sign because I know she won't mind, but I'm going to ask everyone else first.

Myrna steps outside and calls across the street, "Hey, doll! You cleared that with Petra, right?"

"All clear! I'm the official sign painter of Ivydell!"

"Well, of course you are! You are Patrice's granddaughter, after all. Come and do mine next. Then let's take a break together."

"You got it!"

Myrna's sign was so faded it was barely legible. I step back and admire my work. There's no mistaking she lives in Wild Sage now.

I put away my supplies for the day, wash my hands, and go back to Myrna's. She's outside nodding her approval of my work. "You're a natural. We should've known you'd be an artist."

"Not like she was."

"You're not supposed to do everything just like she did. I guarantee Patrice intended for you to be your own person."

"She did. You got wine?"

"Already opened the bottle. You got dirty stories to share?"

"You'd have to give me something stronger than wine for that."

"I have tequila."

I follow her inside. "I was joking. My lips are sealed."

"Not for Stinger, I bet."

"Well, you've seen the man, so . . ."

We laugh ourselves giddy. Drinking with her could be dangerous.

"Hey, before we get tipsy, I want to give you something."

She pops the lid on a storage tub and pulls out a small black box. With a silver logo. Oh, goddess, please don't let this be happening.

"If you don't feel a connection to this piece, we'll pick you out another one, but this felt right."

I have never been more afraid to open a box in my life. A dozen images flash in my brain, each one more disturbing than the last.

The box is too small to hold a replica of the woman being mounted by a deer that comprises the pendant resting against her chest. Small mercies feel big sometimes.

With immeasurable trepidation, I lift the lid.

Oh. It's small. I would wear something this size.

It's a bird. An intricate little bird. And it's not violating or being violated by anyone. It's elegant.

And I feel the most unexpected connection to it.

"Myrna, this is beautiful."

"It's a sparrow. I knew I wanted to gift you one of my pieces, but I wasn't sure which one until I opened that box. It just sang out your name the moment I uncovered it. Well, hot damn, I thought. Sparrow's Song. Of course!"

I've never paid a moment's attention to sparrows, to most any birds. I only ever notice seagulls because it's impossible not to notice them.

"Do sparrows mean something special?"

"Oh, there's so much wonderful symbolism associated with them. You look them up when you get a chance."

She pours me a glass of wine while I put on the necklace.

"Okay, I gave you a present. Now, you give me one. How big is his dick?"

We both cackle, knowing she's only joking.

I hope? Because I'm never discussing Jensen's dick with her. But I really love the silver sparrow she gifted me. I don't have a lot of possessions I treasure, but this will forever be precious to me.

"I didn't know you made pieces like this."

"At one point, I only made pieces like that. I knew I was talented. Skilled. But I didn't stand out. I was in a bookstore in Paris, feeling down, wondering if I'd ever be recognized as an artist, and my eyes landed on a book with an image like the pendant I'm wearing on the cover."

"Did you buy it?"

"No. I was scandalized. The shop owner hurried right over to explain the significance of the symbolism in his haughty French accent."

"He made you see it differently."

"All he did was make me think he was a pretentious prick. I'd seen things like that in art before. Hell, I'd seen things far more provocative. But in galleries. Art shows. Never on a book cover. Face out on the shelf where anyone could be subjected to it. To this day, I don't know why it had such an impact, but it stuck with me."

"What made you want to incorporate that into your jewelry?"

"Over the next year, I kept stumbling across images of humans engaged with animals outside of art on a canvas or illustrations. I saw sculptures. A lamp base one time. Blown glass figures. Surely, those things had always been in front of me. Why had my eyes ignored them before? And why couldn't I stop seeing them after that damn book cover?"

"So, you kept seeing them, and then what?"

"First, I became desensitized. And then I got curious. It was the seventies. Sex was everywhere. All kinds of sex. And I was spending a lot of time in Europe, but I was still a little wet behind the ears."

"And Europe wasn't quite as puritanical as The States."

"To put it mildly. I learned about sex clubs and kink conventions."

"Conventions?"

"Oh, yeah. Conventions with vendors."

"That's where you got recognized."

"Some paths to glory require a detour. I had nothing to lose but time and the cost of materials, so I took a chance. I didn't know if anyone attending that first convention would even be able to afford my stuff. Turned out, a lot of those people had money. And they liked quality items. They saw my pieces as art. And some of them probably just wanted a shocking piece of jewelry. All I knew was they were willing to pay what I was asking. Soon after, I learned the real value of word-of-mouth advertising. That community talked to each other."

"You went on the kink convention circuit?"

"For a little while. And then a gallery in Amsterdam called. One in Paris, where it all began for me. Then London. New York. Philadelphia."

"And the rest was history."

"I rode high for a while. Things shifted considerably in the mid-eighties, but I had a following by then. I refocused on the tamer subjects. Started making things other than jewelry, too. Candlesticks. Vases. Called it jewelry for the home. That had a moment."

"You still make your shocking stuff, though, right? It's your logo."

"Far less of it, but there are collectors. Branching into those pieces taught me the most. Not just about taking risks, but about humanity. Humility. Exposed me to things that broadened my views in ways I'll always be grateful for. That's why I won't be ashamed of it. Not ever."

"You are a complete fucking badass. You know that, right?"

"First thing I tell myself in the mirror every morning."

"I bet Gran thought you were a riot."

"I'm not sure what she thought about me, but I adored her. And your mom."

Myrna insists she has to feed me while we polish off the wine. She makes us grilled cheese sandwiches, says she's a better artist than a cook.

But I think her grilled cheese sandwiches are almost as good as Gran's. Sometimes, the simplest things are the best.

Jensen

Digging Holes

I SEE IVY THROUGH my kitchen window. What is she doing out there? Jesus wept! Who taught her how to use a shovel? She's going to chop her damn foot off.

"You're not trying to dig a hole big enough to hide my body, are you?"

"In the front yard? No. I would definitely do that out back. Your sign is finished."

"Drop the shovel. I'll be right back."

I jog over to the shop to get the auger. Of course, I have to put gas in it. For a damn sign that is completely unnecessary. But I agreed to it. It might've been my idea. The details are fuzzy. A lot of shit is fuzzy in my head right now.

"Stand back." I turn on the auger and let it do the work her shovel couldn't.

She leans over to inspect the first hole. "Hey, that thing's cool. I want to do the other one."

"Maybe next time. Hold that sign up so I can see where to drill the second hole."

I set the auger in the right place and tell her to step away with the sign. Didn't mean to snap, but it's already out of my mouth.

"Somebody needs a nap. Or a snack."

"Is it you, Ivy? Are you somebody?"

"Well, yeah, me, too. But I always need those things."

"True." I make the second hole. "You know the sign needs to be set in concrete, right? It won't stay upright for long with nothing but dirt to hold it in place."

"Do you have concrete?"

I hesitate for a minute. "Yes. But I don't feel like mixing any right now. Just put your sign up, and I'll make it more secure tomorrow."

"Maybe the pots will help in the meantime."

I look around for said pots. "That's just what I need. More flowers to water."

"You're welcome."

She sets her pots in place, and then she stands back up, tilting her head when she looks at me.

"You look like hell. Are you sick?"

"I warned you about that sweet talk."

"Seriously, Jensen, are you okay?"

"I will be."

The wind blows her hair into her eyes, and she swipes it away with the back of her hand so she can see me again. She's worried, and I hate that I'm the reason. But this confirmation that she cares, it matters. I don't want to shit on that.

"Thank you."

"For what?"

"The sign. The flowers. For just being you."

"Don't forget making you dig holes in the desert when you feel like shit."

She always makes me laugh. "I appreciate that most of all."

"Do you need medicine? Soup?"

"No. Just rest."

"Okay, but if you need anything, call me. I really don't mind going to the store for you."

"You have paint in your hair."

"I'll take a shower first."

"Go take your shower. But you don't need to go to the store."

"Call me if I do."

She steps closer to kiss me on the cheek. Then she puts her hand on my forehead to check me for a fever like I'm a little kid. That annoys the piss out of me, so I pull my head back out of her reach. I smell mint. She's sweaty. Her hair is a mess. But she still smells good.

"Okay. I can take a hint. I'll leave you alone to be sick and cranky."

I watch her walk away. There is a voice telling me to call her back, but I know I need to let her go.

I'm no good for anybody right now.

But for her, I want to be.

Her toe catches on a rock, and she stumbles. I'm halfway to the road before I realize she didn't fall. She's fine. Never looks back. Has no idea I was running to help her.

I'm always going to want to run to her. To catch her. Protect her.

The moment I saw her, I knew she was full of complications.

And I ran headfirst into them. Eyes wide-the-fuck-open. I knew. I knew exactly what was going to happen as soon as I asked her if she was lost, and she looked at me with those eyes.

I was the one who was lost. But I was supposed to find her.

It's time to find me again.

Ivy
Don't Blink

I CAN'T SLEEP. I keep thinking I should text Jensen to check on him, but he recoiled when I touched his forehead to see if he had a fever. He hated that. I'm guessing he wouldn't love a well check in the middle of the night, either. I hope he's sleeping. And doesn't have a fever.

Dammit. I hate knowing he's a jerk when he's sick. Why are the best people always the worst when they're sick?

Mom says it's true about injuries, too. The patients who are the hardest to deal with when they come into the ER are sometimes the most grateful by the time they leave. It's usually the ones accustomed to taking care of other people, so it's hard for them to accept they're not in charge of their own situation. The people who are always looking ahead, trying to plan and keep the path clear for everyone else, to protect the people they love.

When they get hurt or sick, they feel like they've failed, even when they had no fault at all in their own injury or illness.

I get it, but it still pisses me off. He should've let me help him. Now I'm wide awake and doom-scrolling when I should be sleeping.

Zara just posted something. She's awake, too. I wonder if she's thought anymore about seeing Ivydell in person. She was probably just typing her random thoughts with no serious intent, but I wouldn't mind if she came to visit before I left. Might be nice to have someone at home who would get it when I talked about this place.

And I am undoubtedly going to talk about it until people are sick of hearing it. Some of them will think I'm making up parts of my stories, the way I always thought Mom and Gran were.

Zara probably already thinks I'm crazy for being here. Soooo . . . it probably won't make anything worse if I bring it up again.

> *Hey, I was serious when I said you should come check out Ivydell.*

> *Why are you awake? Where's your desert dude?*

> *Sick. And not in the mood for a nurse.*

> *Oh, he's one of those people.*

> *Yeah. Wanna meet him?*

> *Stop tempting me. I've met me. I might just show up.*

> *You could come for the festival.*

> *When is it?*

> *First weekend in April.*

I don't have any plans.

I'm looking up the closest airport. I'll get back to you.

I'd probably drive. You drove it.

It's nine hours.

So? I can drive nine hours.

She'd drive nine hours to visit me in the middle of nowhere? Holy shit. We might be better friends than I thought. Well, damn. What else have I missed?

Jensen

Hard Labor

CUJO'S FRONT TIRE STOPS a few feet from the wheelbarrow I'm standing over. He shuts off his bike but doesn't dismount. "Damn. Breaking rocks in the hot sun. Is this your penance?"

"I'm not breaking rocks. I'm mixing concrete."

"Making me some new shoes? You plan on pushing me out of a boat?"

"Not today. But I'd sleep with one eye open if I were you."

"No. If you were me, you wouldn't be worried at all. What's the concrete for?"

"For the sign. Ivy made it. Apparently, *Jojo* helped." I cock an eyebrow when I look up at him.

"You trying to bait me into knocking that smirk off your face?"

"I'm just trying to stay busy."

"Let me know when you're done. We'll get some fishing in before you decide to pave the roads."

"You buy a boat, by any chance?"

"No. You'll have to shove me off the bank."

"Good thing I started lifting again."

"We'll do some more of that after you clean all our fish."

"I'll clean *my* fish."

"Welcome back, you cocky little bastard."

"I'm getting there." I scoop concrete into a hole. "I might owe you more than cleaning fish could repay."

"You don't owe me shit. I'll be back in a few hours."

I set the sign in place and smooth out the top of the concrete around the posts. I could've left it messy. Nobody around here would've cared. Except Ivy. She'll want it to look nice.

Besides, I intentionally over-poured so I could spread out the excess. It gives the flower pots a level place to sit. If I don't smooth it out, it defeats the purpose.

The concrete hasn't cured enough to put the pots on it by the time Cujo comes back, but I've set them on the ground between the posts, so if Ivy happens by, she'll know I didn't forget. I told her I'd secure the posts, and I did.

"The flowers are a nice touch. They match your eyes."

"Shut up and get in the truck."

The wind tries to blow us off the bank a few times, but we wait it out and keep fishing. We manage to pull a couple of fish out of the water before we're done. There was another pair of guys out here when we threw our lines in, but they gave up and went home before they got a bite. Ran off before the chop eased up.

Their pillowcases won't feel rough against their windburned cheeks tonight. They probably called us dumbasses while they were loading up to leave. But we're the ones having fresh fish for dinner because we didn't give up.

Cujo takes his second fish off the hook, and we call it.

"Sometimes, it pays to be hardheaded." He tosses the fish into the cooler with the others.

The wind picks up again. It'll blow this way all night, off and on, gusting and then going quiet until you almost forget about it. "My dad used to say stubborn and stupid were the same thing, that you couldn't be one without being both. He believed he was neither. I spent a long time thinking he was an asshole on purpose, that he worked at it. Now, I catch myself thinking he was just stupidly stubborn. And for what?"

I know I can be stubborn, but I'm not stupid. I know when to wait out the wind and when to cut bait.

Cujo nods like he's mulling over what I've said. "There were plenty of times I didn't understand why my old man did the things he did."

"Every boy hits that stage where he thinks he's smarter than his father, but it sucks to be a grown man and realize you were right. You're supposed to look back and see that he was a wiser man than you thought. Mine wasn't."

"You can't pick your parents. But you don't have to repeat their mistakes."

"I don't want to be a damn thing like my dad." I slide my tackle box into the bed of my truck and slam the tailgate. "But I don't think I'm mad at him anymore. I don't know what I feel."

I'll always be mad he took Jenna, but that anger feels less like an active volcano now. More like the hardened lava of a past eruption. It's still there, and it probably always will be. Not dangerous anymore, but a permanent reminder of how fast things can go wrong.

"Maybe you're done with being weighed down. Tired of just existing. Ready to live again."

"Might be long overdue."

"There's no deadline. Getting there is all that matters."

Cujo and I lift for a while as soon as we get back to Ivydell. I think we both know we won't do it if we wait until after we eat. I don't comment on how much weight he puts on the bar. And he doesn't try to shame me into adding more.

He lights the grill behind my shop, and I grab us some cold beers from my fridge. If I offered him a glass of wine, he might shank me with the corkscrew.

Some nights, a meal you've eaten hundreds of times before tastes better than it ever has. The food's the same. But it's better.

Ivy

An Angel at First Glance

SINCE I'VE BEEN TRYING not to smother Jensen, I've been showering Mom with updates about my time here. She seems genuinely glad to hear all about it. That date she didn't tell me anything about before is now referred to as their first date. She's gone out with him three more times, and those dates have been the subject of her last three texts.

This is an unprecedented level of dating for her. When I was growing up, she always tried to tell me she believed in the third date policy, meaning no kissing until then. When I was sixteen, I asked her why she didn't follow that policy if she believed in it. Her eyes looked like they were going to bulge out of their sockets. I explained that if the story about the magician who fathered me was true, they definitely did not go on four dates, and they definitely did more than kiss.

There was no further mention of the third date policy in our house, but as I sit here texting her, I can't help but giggle about how she's now been on four dates with this guy. I guess they've kissed. For all I know, he could be snoring in her bed right now.

I'm happy for her, so I don't give her a hard time. I will, but I'll wait until I know he's a good guy.

Jensen texted me a few times yesterday, but he didn't ask to see me. He told me he secured the posts for his sign, but I'd already seen it when I went to the store.

I mentioned that the concrete has eroded around a lot of the other signs. The little dots that indicate someone is typing kept appearing and disappearing, making me laugh because I could envision what he was doing: Sighing. Typing a message to say he was not repairing everyone's signs. Then backspacing. Saying he'd take a look at them. Backspacing again. Saying he'd shore up the ones that were in danger of falling down, but that was it.

It's what he does when his knee-jerk reaction is no. He softens his stance a few times, and then he settles on a compromise. With himself. He talks his way around it until it's his idea. It might be one of my favorite things about him. Maybe because so many things about him are still unknown to me, but I know I can count on that. He doesn't guard that part of himself so closely.

I painted a few more signs yesterday afternoon, and I kept hoping maybe Jensen would wander up to check the posts, but he didn't. I didn't hear from him last night. He said he was feeling better in his last text message, though.

We've talked about being open to seeing each other after I went back home. I still want to try that, but I'm not sure if he's into the idea anymore. Maybe distancing himself now is his way of softening the blow when the subject comes up again. I don't think I'm brave enough to bring it back up. If his answer is no, I'd rather just leave and let things fade out between us.

If that makes me a coward, then that's what I am. But I don't want to see his eyes if he tells me he no longer thinks we'd be worth the effort. Maybe it's more that I don't want him to see my eyes if that happens.

It's possible he's just been tired from being sick.

But Josephine mentioned he went fishing with Cujo. I think she thought I already knew. Hopefully, my face didn't reveal too much. If he felt well enough to fish, he couldn't have been all that tired.

There is a faint knock on my door. I think that was a knock?

It's Alma and Elma. Their hair is braided and they're wearing matching beige linen pants with lightweight blue sweaters. Alma's is navy, and Elma's is the color of the sky. No puffy vests today.

"Good morning, dear."

"We thought you might be ready to walk down for coffee. Leo is brewing the mushrooms today, and we remembered you were keen to try it."

Keen? I wouldn't go that far, but I didn't gag like some people did when he mentioned it.

"Let me slip on some shoes." I run my fingers through my hair and pull it up into a loose bun. I'm not really ready to go anywhere, but it's sweet that they came by, so I'm going, anyway.

"This is for you." Alma holds out a small organza bag when I step outside to join them.

"Just a little token of appreciation."

"What did I do to deserve it?"

"You spiffed up our sign. And it looks so nice."

"It'll make it easier for people to find us."

"I was happy to do it." I open the bag. It's a chunk of amethyst, but it's been carved. I pull it out to take a better look. It's an angel. She looks like she's swaying.

"Thank you. This reminds me of Gran's angels in her paintings."

"We thought you'd like that one."

"I do. I like it very much."

All I planned to take away from this place were memories, and hopefully, some answers. But these little gifts I've been given mean so much. They're nice things, but they're heartfelt, too.

"Let me just put her inside real quick. I'll have to find a special place for her later."

"She wants to sit next to your bed, dear."

Yeah, the hairs on the back of my neck heard that. What the fuck? She wants to? Okay, then.

I slip back inside and set her on the nightstand, but I turn her so she faces the kitchen, not my bed. There are some things I just don't think angels need to watch over. At least I hope there will be more action not meant for an angel's eyes over the next month.

"Ready to go," I say, and we set off at a very leisurely pace. The mushroom brew should be good and strong by the time we get there. The Spirit Sisters do not rush.

"Does the angel have a name?" I think they'll say I can name her whatever I want, but it seems rude not to ask. I can't explain that. These women always make me feel like I've shown up to class after not doing the assigned reading and am silently praying the teacher won't call on me. And feeling guilty because I don't even know who I'm praying to. Like hoping to win the lottery while knowing you didn't bother with buying a ticket. You know it doesn't work like that, but desperate times . . .

"Her name is Hilda."

No. What? That's not angelic. Hilda is getting a new name. There's no way around it.

"She won't mind if you change it," Elma says. Probably not

because she could hear my thoughts.

Jensen makes a beeline for me as soon as I enter the community center. "You really don't want to try that mushroom coffee. Trust me. Hold your cup out to Tawny instead of Leo. She has regular coffee."

"I already told Leo I'd try it. You look like you feel better."

"I do."

He walks with me to the counter, trying to change my mind with his eyes pulling toward Tawny when I stretch my hand toward Leo. I'm not going back on my word.

It's not as bad as the first mushroom coffee I tried. This one has some chocolate in it. You can taste it, but it doesn't drown out the earthy bitterness of the mushrooms. I drink it, anyway. If all the stuff Leo's rattled off about it is true, I should have superpowers for the rest of the day.

Not to mention the sugar from Tawny's special breakfast bars. No granola, plenty of brown sugar and cinnamon. And butter. They're so rich and gooey and sweet that I could eat the whole pan.

I tell Tawny I'll stick around and help them wash dishes, but she won't let me.

"You're sweet to offer, but hosting the coffee shop is something Leo and I do because we want to. That includes cleaning up and reorganizing after everybody's done. This is a gift from us to our neighbors. You just accept it and go on with your day, knowing you don't owe us anything."

"Okay. If you're sure."

Everyone is disbursing, and I'm stalling. Jensen is still hanging around. He looks more delicious than those breakfast bars. If he keeps putting distance between us now, I'll know it has nothing to do with him being sick.

He catches up to me when I head for the door. "Can I walk you home?"

"Sure."

I'm not usually at a loss for words around him, but I can't think of a single thing to say as we walk away from the community center.

A car I've never seen drives past. Jensen waves. "April's back. I hope Petra is prepared for that."

"What do you mean?"

"She can be a little high maintenance." He looks to the sky the way some people do when a plane flies over, but there's nothing up there. Not even a bird. "Maybe she won't be this year."

"Yeah, some people mellow with age."

He looks at me as if I've handed him a hammer when he asked for a hairbrush, but then he quickly wipes the expression from his face, nodding as if he agrees with me. "Yeah. Some do."

I'm missing something here, but I assume I'll understand after I get to know April.

I know I don't have to ask Jensen if he wants to come in when we reach Sparrow's Song. There may not have been many words passing between us, but the sexual tension has been heavy.

And however badly he wants to stay for a while, I want him here even more.

His eyes roam around my space like he's searching for something.

"What are you looking for?"

"Just taking in your chaos."

"I just cleaned!"

"Why are there always dirty clothes on your floor?"

"Like I had space in my car on the way here for a hamper."

"You have a laundry basket. I've seen it."

"Yeah, and it still has some of the same laundry in it."

"So, you can't put your dirty clothes in your laundry basket because you never put away your clean clothes from when you did laundry at my place."

"Exactly. And when the basket is empty, I'll put all the dirty clothes in it and go to the laundromat."

"You don't have to do that. I'll scare the lizards off for you again. But you should buy a second basket, so you have one for clean clothes and one for dirty clothes. They're stackable. Two won't take up much more space than one."

"Quit trying to trick me into becoming a neat freak like you."

"I don't know what I was thinking."

"Are you thinking about kissing me at some point today?"

"How about now? Would now be a good time?"

He advances on me with a theatrical swagger, running a hand through his hair, narrowing his eyes, licking his lips, and . . . no, he did not just roll his hips like that. He's ridiculous.

I try not to laugh, knowing I'm already losing.

He extends his hand, and when I take it, he stares at me with his eyes wide open. When he pulls me forward, he lifts my hand and kisses my fingers. I've never had my hand kissed as much as he does it. If ever. I wouldn't have found that hot if someone had described it happening to them, but when it happens to me, it's more than his lips grazing my fingers. It's an imprint—as lasting as if his lips had been tattooed there.

When he brings me closer to kiss my mouth, I'm already on fire for him. His tongue sweeps over mine as he walks me back toward my bed. I bump into the nightstand, knocking over the amethyst angel who needs a new name. It startles me, causes me to break our kiss.

I turn to rescue Hilda, and Jensen looks over my shoulder. "Where'd she come from?"

"The Spirit Sisters gave her to me this morning. I guess they thought I needed an angel."

"Are you sure she's not supposed to be a ghost? If that's an angel, where are her wings?"

"Oh, shit." I turn the figure around in my fingers. "Why'd I think she was an angel?"

"I asked you first."

She has no wings. I could've sworn she did. I guess it was just the long dress and long, flowing hair that made me assume angel. But she could be a ghost. A witch? My fingers release her like she's burst into flames. She bounces against my mattress. "What the hell is she?"

"Well, she's probably pissed off right now because you just threw her like that."

I snatch her up. "I didn't throw her. I just dropped her. On accident."

"You probably shouldn't let her know you're afraid of her."

"I'm not afraid of her. She's not real."

"Are you sure? Because I can see her."

"She's a real rock, but she's not alive. Or undead. She can't hurt me."

He crosses his forearms in front of his face defensively.

"Stop that!" I set whatever she is back on my nightstand. Gently. But facing the kitchen. "You're mean."

He drops his arms. "You're beautiful. Come here."

"Are you going to be nice?"

"So nice."

We shed our clothes in record time. I crawl under the covers. The sheets are soft against my skin. Sensual.

"Under the covers?" he asks.

"You've seen every inch of me. I like to be under the covers sometimes."

"You sure snuggling under the covers isn't too mushy for you?"

"I trust you to keep things depraved enough for my comfort."

His mouth closes on mine. It's a deep kiss, the kind he specializes in. He kneads my scalp like he's trying to put me to sleep. But there's no way he'd let me drift off with this hard-on between us. I circle my fingers around it. They don't quite touch, but I'm covering enough skin to make him shudder when I slide my hand down a few inches.

"I love that I can make you do that."

"I love that you can make me do that."

His hand slips between my legs. "And I love the way your pussy feels in my hand, the way it tastes, the sound you make when I first push inside you . . ."

"Make me make sounds, Jensen."

"I'm going to make love to you, Ivy Dell McAdams."

"Just Ivy."

"Wild Ivy."

"That doesn't exist in the desert."

"Yes, she does."

His fingers push inside me, and I make a sound.

He kisses me, and the sound escapes my mouth again. It's not the one he referred to earlier, the gasp that leaves me the moment his cock enters my pussy.

This is different, something between a moan and a cry for mercy. It's needy, laced with desperation. But only I know that beyond being desperate for everything we're about to do, I'm twice as desperate not to feel the warm comfort that will linger when we're done.

But the need for what comes before is too strong to stop it from happening. The fear of what comes after is a consequence I'll have to face. Again. And again. Until I get over it. I think if anyone could get me over it, it's Jensen James Stinger.

He pulls the covers completely over our heads.

His cock stretches my opening.

I gasp. And then I relax and let him make love to me.

He'll be rough again later. But right now, he's pure comfort. And I could be okay with needing this. Someday.

"Goddamn, your pussy feels good. I love the way your tight little snatch milks my cock."

"Those are awfully dirty words from a man who's supposed to be making love to me."

"I can't help it. You make me want to make dirty love."

"You think you can just lure me in with soft touches and sweet words, and then whisper filthy things in my ear as soon as I let my guard down?"

"How about if I keep the touches soft?" His thumb coasts over my nipple with the slightest contact he can manage.

"Tease."

"Is that what I'm doing? Am I teasing you?" He pushes his hips forward until he's balls-deep and grinding slowly. "What do you want me to do to you?"

"Kiss me."

"Whenever you want. Wherever you want."

He starts with my mouth, moves down to kiss my nipples, spending enough time on each one to have me grinding with him. His hot mouth kisses between my ribs, and then he pulls his dick out of me entirely. No re-entry thrust follows. He kisses his way down the center of my torso. His warm breath tickles my abdomen and makes me squirm.

I'm obscenely wet. Good thing he never minds making a mess. His mouth reaches my pussy. And he makes a sound.

I shove the covers down until his shoulders are exposed so I can watch him devouring me.

My thighs strain to draw together, but he pushes them apart. They shake uncontrollably as I come on his perfect tongue while he kisses my clit. Shamelessly.

He pushes my knees to my shoulders and guides his dick back into me until he's fully sheathed. His thrusts are forceful, gaining speed. But I know there is still going to be a lingering warm comfort when he's done. Because it's him. It's us.

And we can't fuck without familiarity anymore. Not without feeling.

I look into his eyes, and I see it.

He shudders.

Seizes.

Shatters.

His orgasm is tempestuous, and I love watching him ride it out.

He releases my legs and lowers his body onto mine. Exhausted limbs. Ragged breathing. Neither one of us is going to win any productivity awards today.

He brings me a towel, and he lies down on top of the comforter, still breathing hard.

When I come back from the bathroom, I crawl under the covers, and he joins me. Holds me with my head cradled in the crook of his shoulder. Snuggles me close.

"This feels a little mushy."

"Go to sleep, you dirty whore."

"Thank you."

He kisses the top of my head. "Anything for you, beautiful."

I OPEN MY EYES, and the amethyst figure on my nightstand stares back at me.

Dammit, Jensen.

I turn her toward the kitchen again so I don't have to look at her O-shaped mouth, like she's shocked beyond belief by what's taken place in this bed in broad daylight.

"Haha," I say, rolling over to face him.

"Don't laugh at me. I'm sensitive."

"When did you turn her around? I never even knew you got out of bed."

"I didn't. I slept like a rock."

"Better be careful calling her a rock. Next time you put your fingers on her, she might bite you."

"I'm telling you, I've been in this bed the whole time."

"Okay, sure. Whatever you say."

He rolls on top of me. "Really? Anything?"

I steal a quick sideways glance to be sure we're not being watched anymore because I don't know what this man might say next. But I know there's a good chance I'm going to say yes to whatever he proposes.

Also from INDIE SPARKS

Steamy Rom-Com Duologies:

VENGEFUL VIXENS:

Your Boss Says Hi!

She's only looking for a rebound guy, but her ex's boss plays for keeps. He's a former NFL player who used to have thousands of women screaming his name every week. Now, he only wants one woman to scream his name, and she just might become his biggest fan yet.

Your Trainer Says Hi!

She only wants to see her ex's beloved personal trainer in the gym—until he convinces her his hot tub could do wonders for her aching muscles. He isn't wrong, but between the heat, the bubbles, and his off-the-clock skills, she might be in too deep before she knows it. He's definitely not her type. So, why can't she stop seeing him?

NAUGHTY AT THE NOUVEAU:

Maintenance & Management

She's the new property manager. He's the new maintenance supervisor. They rub each other the wrong way . . . until they start to rub each other so very right. There's a non-fraternization policy, so they really shouldn't. But there's only one bed!

Landscaping & Leasing

He ghosted her after an unfortunate incident that she had absolutely no control over—and now, she's accidentally hired his landscaping company. She may not be completely immune to his charms (that voice!), but she's not weak enough to fall for him twice. But what if she doesn't know the whole story about why he disappeared from her life?

More Small Town Romance:

Peri

They were the wildest couple in town once, but that was a long time ago. They're not restless small-town kids anymore. And she's not back in town to see him. But seeing him once won't hurt anything. How much trouble could they get into as adults? Hardly any if you disregard the dirty karaoke and the lewd (allegedly) graffiti . . . and that old flame reigniting like an inferno.